A NEW WORD FOR MURDER

Abby Irish
luck is a feeling

Susie,
No 4-leaf clover
in the desert. :)
Abby Iris

MORTON L. KURLAND MD

ABBY KURLAND IRISH

ISBN 978-1-961017-83-2 (Paperback)
ISBN 978-1-961017-84-9 (Ebook)

Inquiries and Book Orders should be addressed to:

Leavitt Peak Press
17901 Pioneer Blvd Ste L #298, Artesia, California 90701
Phone #: 2092191548

Contents

Introduction

There is a skein of madness which runs through the taking of a human life. It can be likened to a blood red thread which appears in the fabric of every case of a capital crime. If you look into it carefully, it is always there. It rises sometimes quickly and obviously like a great crimson salmon rising to the lure of a animal hiding in a dark cave.

Since psychiatrists believe that all human behavior can be explained, there should be a way to understand the mind of a murderer. It is the purpose of this book to explore this book to explore the hidden recesses in the minds of several murderers who have committed their lethal crimes in the otherwise magical surroundings of the Palm Springs desert resort area. They, like Cain, have committed the ultimate crime, murder in paradise.

The job of a forensic psychiatrist is to assist either the court or the prosecuting attorney or the defense attorney in understanding something about the motives, the intent and the possible mitigating circumstances involved in a crime. In a capital crime, such as a murder, this of course becomes even more essential in view of the potential sentence and the enormity of the responsibility of both the jury and the judge in dealing with somebody who has been adjudged to have taken human life. The job of the psychiatrist then becomes important in ferreting out the unconscious motivations, the intent or lack of it involved in the killing and what possibly has led this individual or group of individuals to the ultimate crime.

Since Palm Springs, California is seen as a rather unique place, it is sometimes surprising to other people that this kind of activity would go on in such an idyllic setting.

People have preconceived notions about almost everything. What it is like to be a king or a queen or a hero or heroine are some. How it is to be fabulously wealthy or to be a movie star are others.

Being a psychiatrist in Palm Springs, California, must mean treating a special kind of person in a special setting. Maybe it means seeing patients on a chaise lounge, near a pool, or making house calls at a Xanadu-like palace. Maybe not.

I am a board-certified psychiatrist, and have been practicing in the Palm Springs, California, community since 1971. Prior to that, I practiced for ten years in the New York City metropolitan area. In returning east to visit friends and in meeting people from other parts of the country at meetings and conventions, I frequently am asked to discuss the quality and nature of my practice in the fabulous desert resort community. Most people know that Palm Springs is the golf capitol of the world. It has more swimming pools per capita than any place else on the face of the globe. This, plus the fact that movie stars and millionaires have been living in the desert during the winters for more than half a century, gives people a glamorous, glittering and tinseled view of "the desert." In discussions about Palm Springs, outsiders always are interested in knowing if I have seen any movie stars or TV personalities, or the like, in practice. They expect that a successful psychiatric practice is built around millionaires and captains of industry, heirs to fabulous fortunes and bored wives of the robber barons of our society. The recent publicity given to the many prominent theatrical people at the Betty Ford Center, which is located in Rancho Mirage at the Eisenhower Medical Center, has added to this notion of our community as being a magnet which attracts the rich and famous, both for living and for medical care.

When I inform friends, colleagues and acquaintances that in addition to a traditional psychiatric practice, I have been engaged in a significant number of medical/legal cases and court consultations, they are surprised. When they discover that I have examined more than twenty murder suspects for the purposes of court evaluation in the past few years, they appear to be shocked. How can someone commit murder in Palm Springs? It is as though one were telling them that murder was committed in Paradise. Even this, of course, has historic precedent. It is true that Cain killed Abel in the Garden of Eden. If Cain could do it to Abel, then John can do it to Mary, or Mary can do it to John in Palm Springs. And they do.

The remainder of this book is devoted to a discussion of not only how, when and where these murders were committed but, more importantly, why. Is there a connection among them? What is the common theme in each? People are always interested in the details of murder cases. Detective magazines and books, newspapers and periodicals are filled with the latest gory, bloody, violent, intricate, unusual and surprising cases of someone doing in someone else. This is included in the stories that have been told to me by the accused perpetrators of these crimes. In addition, part of my job has been to try to understand 'why'. This can be for the benefit of the court, which has appointed me to get some information on the mental status of the accused, or the district attorney, or the defense attorney. They need to know more about why these events might have happened and what the motivations for the killings may have been. 'Why' usually presents a story in itself, which is often as interesting, or more interesting, than the details of 'how'. It is more meaningful to the rest of us in terms of understanding how things can go wrong even in the Garden of Eden, and how even ordinary people can be sucked into a situation which is far beyond their control and often resulting in the ultimate destruction of human life. There is some common denominator and, like a detective, the forensic psychiatrist's job is to seek it out.

There is always more than one reason for every form of human behavior. It has been said in the psychiatric literature that human behavior is multifaceted and multidetermined. That means that even the simplest things, such as what you eat for breakfast, how much you eat, where and when you eat it is determined by a whole series of factors. You can be on a diet and try to eat only cornflakes and skimmed milk. You can be filled with anxiety and agitation and consume four eggs, four pieces of toast, six strips of bacon, hashed brown potatoes, orange juice, coffee, and a sweet roll, and be the same person. You can be in a hurry to get to work and gulp down a cup of coffee, or you can be trying to while away time and dawdle over the same cup. You can be busy talking to a friend or a loved one, and not bother eating your food, or you can be so preoccupied with devouring it that you don't know that anyone else is even around. There are literally hundreds of reasons for even the simplest kind of human behavior, and when one considers the most violent form of human behavior, these reasons are even more complex and multiple. I will try to outline a few of the common reasons in several of the cases to be discussed, understanding that there are always more details than I can possibly include and that these are, in some degree, important as well.

I should mention to home town readers of this book that I have, in fact, changed the names and some of the easily identifiable facts of these cases. These are all real cases and all real people whom I saw in my capacity as a member of the Psychiatric Panel for the Riverside County Superior Court or as a consulting psychiatrist, both in the Office of the Public Defender, the District Attorney's Office and private attorneys in Southern California. It was my feeling that it would be useful to disguise the identities of the perpetrators and the victims in order to protect others. Many people, especially friends and families of perpetrators, as well as victims, would like to live down the dramatic and sensationalized events of the past. Newspaper and television media have filled their plates with the spotlight of public scrutiny. My interest here is to tell the stories of the motives and feelings of the individuals involved and not to expose innocent but related people to further pain and scrutiny. That is why I have, in fact, made efforts to protect these people by giving different names and dates and locales in each instance. I have, of course, attempted to maintain the integrity of the ideas, motivations and feelings of the protagonists, and think that I have in fact been faithful to this effort.

CHAPTER 1

The Freeway Murders

Killings, even the most wanton and senseless appearing on the surface, all have motives. Police authorities seek out the motives for the killings and, thereby, have a much easier time in discovering the identity of the murderer. People usually kill for a reason, and if you can discover what they have to gain and what their thinking was prior to the killing, you can usually discover the identity of the murderer. Most murders are committed by people who know their victims. Not only do they know them, but they usually know them very well. Often, they are related, husband and wife, father and son, and the like. Sometimes they are business partners. Sometimes they are lovers, but they usually are close and have frequent contact. When the killer becomes an unknown spectre in the night and when the motive is hard to fathom, the detective work becomes more difficult, and the job of apprehending the killer can be a very tough one indeed.

An unknown assailant attacking in the middle of the night on a group of unsuspecting victims is a situation that we all dread. It is much as if we were flying on a commercial airline for a holiday trip when hijackers take ever. Imagine the scenario in the following case:

A middle-aged couple is driving east on Interstate Highway 10, heading from Los Angeles to Arizona, on a summer evening. It has cooled off considerably from the over one hundred degrees of desert heat during the day, and the air is becoming pleasant and even balmy. They decide to turn off the air-conditioning and open the windows

1

to get some fresh air. As they are driving along, they don't actually notice an unremarkable brown Chevrolet that is coming up behind them. Both of the windows on the two-door car are wide open. The driver sits peering ahead. He is looking at all of the cars in front of him, expecting to see one with windows open and the dashboard lights on in the fading light of a late summer evening. They drive along talking about where they are going to stop for a snack or a cup of coffee, or possibly about how they will visit their relatives in Northern Arizona and surprise them with a home-baked bundt cake.

The brown Chevy pulls up alongside of the middle-aged couple's car, and starts to parallel it in speed. As the man and wife sit there talking to each other and looking forward at the road, they don't actually notice the driver of the Chevy pick-up, holding a large double-barreled shotgun aiming it through the window at them. The only thing that they really perceive is a loud, crashing noise and the driver pitching forward, as he is hit by a load of buckshot and killed instantly. The wife is also struck by several pellets. She manages to survive the ensuing crash because they haven't been going very fast, and the car rolls off the road into a ditch on the side of the freeway.

The brown Chevy continues on, heading east, accelerating to sixty miles an hour, the driver waiting to find another car with an open window and the dashboard lights lit. And he found another and another and another.

This scene actually occurred in California some time ago. There were six victims finally who were actually killed, and at least eleven others who were injured, either in being struck by pellets from the shotgun, or in the ensuing auto crash when the driver was killed or injured.

Why would anybody want to drive along a freeway and randomly kill people in one blood-spattered evening? The immediate thought is: "He has to be crazy" and, of course, in the broadest sense of the word, one has to agree. But, crazy in what way? Crazy in what direction? And what do we mean by crazy?

These are questions which had to be answered and which the court and the attorneys in dealing with this case put to a number of

2

psychiatrists. I was among them, and these are some of the facts which I gathered and some of the answers which I proposed.

Charles Baxter was a twenty-nine-year-old, white male, unemployed factory worker-, who was finally apprehended near the Arizona border in Blythe, California, at the end of his freeway spree. He had already decided to surrender to the authorities when he saw a cordon of Highway Patrol cars strung across Interstate 10 outside of Blythe, as the sun rose on the morning following the murders and bloody injuries which he had inflicted all through the night, driving east from Los Angeles towards Arizona.

Actually, most of the shootings had occurred between the towns of Banning and Desert Center, an area which mainly includes the Coachella Valley of California. The Coachella Valley is the site of the famed desert resorts of Palm Springs, Rancho Mirage, LaQuinta, Palm Desert, Indian Wells and all of the golf courses, swimming pools, and fabulous estates in those communities.

Charley Baxter had never seen any of the golf courses, never swam in any of the swimming pools and never even came near the fabulous estates in the Valley. Charley Baxter was born and raised in the city of Los Angeles. He was one of a number of children who were born to his mother, Mary Elizabeth Baxter. Mary Elizabeth had, at various times, to been Mary Elizabeth Baxter, and she had also been Mary Elizabeth Sims, and Mary Elizabeth Johnson, and Mary Elizabeth LaRusso, and possibly several others that Charley didn't know about. She had had somewhere between eight and ten children. Again, that wasn't clear; because it got kind of mixed up when Charley was growing up. His mother had had two or three husbands, or at least men who had given her children before his father came along. His father only lasted for a year or two, so he really never knew him, and there were several other men who followed. In addition, some of the men who had come had left children to be cared for by Mary Elizabeth, and she began

not to know the difference between which ones were hers and which ones were his and which ones were theirs, as time went on. No matter how you looked at it, it was a chaotic household in which to be raised.

Charley later said that there was always enough to eat and enough shelter from the elements. The elements, of course, in Los Angeles mainly were rain on some few occasions during the year and some chilliness at night. They never considered the oppressive heat from time to time to be important, and there never was any air-conditioning to be had, except when the kids went to the supermarket and ran around inside the store until the manager kicked them out.

Charley grew up in a sort of nursery school at home atmosphere without supervision. He went to school mainly because the other kids his age were going to school and because his mother wanted to get as many of the kids out of the house as was practical and possible. He never learned very much in school. He never really liked it there anyhow. Later on, when he was in custody on one of many occasions during his adolescence, the "head doctors" suggested that he had something called dyslexia. Charley, to the day of his being arrested for murder, never really knew what dyslexia meant.

It was suggested to Charley's mother that he be placed in some special classes because he had real difficulty in reading the way normal people do.

Instead of reading from left to right, Charley read from right to left. This would have been all right if he were reading Hebrew or Arabic, and it possibly might have helped if he were reading Japanese or Chinese. Unfortunately, he was asked to read English, and he couldn't do so. It probably wouldn't have made any difference because if he were Chinese, Arab or Hebrew, he probably would have read from left to right instead of from right to left. Dyslexics, unfortunately, have the problem of seeing things in the opposite kinds of ways than do others who read normally. This, of course, makes it almost impossible for them to keep up in school and certainly impossible for them to do homework.

Most dyslexics, if they pay attention, are able to listen in class and understand what is going on. They can get by that way for a number of years in grade school anyway, and sometimes can correct these problems with proper training and careful study. Charley, of course, had no training and no study, and his parent (the father had long since gone) was disinterested in pursuing this matter further. It is questionable, according to him, if she knew which one of the men around was his father in the first place. Besides that, it was questionable sometimes in his mind if she knew who he was compared to the other kids in the family. In any event, he never did get any special classes nor special training. He always felt inadequate, incompetent and "just plain stupid" in school. As a result, he became somewhat of a truant, and eventually his mother told the authorities that he was incorrigible. This was probably, from Charley's point of view, not so bad because he then didn't have to go to regular school anymore.

Charley was sent on a number of occasions to the Juvenile Hall. He didn't like that either, because there were all kinds of rules there and no fun. And they still wanted him to learn things. Later, he went to a boys' camp which was run by the California Youth Authority. These days there are no more reform schools.

There are Youth Authority centers and camps and retraining facilities. That is what they call reform schools now. Essentially, they are schools, or training centers or places to warehouse young children whom their families cannot handle. The people who work there are very concerned about dealing with kids like Charley, and do make a real effort to help them. Unfortunately, there are so many of these kinds of kids and so few of the workers, they don't always get very far. To make it even worse, there are many, many kids in these places who have subtle developmental and physical disorders that can't be simply changed by educational methods.

In any event, in Charley's case, he wasn't able to learn very much, and he did wind up finally, at the age of sixteen, being released from one of the Youth Authority centers and being out on his own in the big city.

At around age seventeen, Charley wandered off to Arizona, and spent several years in Phoenix. He said that while in Phoenix he got involved in a number of drug-related activities. It was there that he met people whom he thought to be "in the mob." Whether this is true or not, we probably never will know, but it was his belief that he got in "bad" with them. He was a very small-time runner and a very small-time pusher of drugs to kids in high school.

Sometimes he even worked the junior high school when he was between the ages of seventeen and twenty-one.

Charley managed to make enough to supply himself with his favorite substances, which were amphetamines. On occasion, he tried other drugs, such as sleeping pills and tranquilizers and even heroin and other narcotics. But he never really liked "downers," and he didn't try to use them very often. He always preferred to use "speed."

"Speed" is the kind of thing that made Charley feel good. Amphetamines were his most favorite drug, and he got ahold of them as often as possible. He really liked to use Methedrine, and he would try to get it in its crystalline form as often as possible. He would then be able to shoot it up in his veins by dissolving it in warm water or sniff it in his nose. "Snorting" the substance into the mucous membranes of his nose gave a very rapid absorption without the trouble of using a needle. He, on rare occasions, also got ahold of some Cocaine almost as much as Methedrine, but the Methedrine lasted longer, and it was the kind of "high" that Charley preferred.

Charley didn't really take much notice of whether or not the substances were affecting his brain in any permanent way. The only effect that he wanted and appreciated was the one where it caused him to feel great and happy and energetic. It did all of these things and more. It gradually destroyed the tissue of his cerebral cortex. But let's hold that for a moment.

Charley began to feel that maybe he could do even better with acquiring money and drugs if he didn't have to spend so much on his suppliers. They took so much of his cash away that they only left him a small profit. He finally began raising his own prices to his customers and eventually saving a little bit of his greater profit by not turning it over to his suppliers. Eventually, he withheld about fifteen hundred dollars from someone who had given him drugs, and kept it for himself. He realized that this was a rather dangerous business. He knew that people, at the very least, could have their arms and legs broken for withholding money from higher ups in the drug business. Foreseeing this possible business setback and short fall in his anticipated cash flow as far as the supplier was concerned, he decided to discretely close down his operation. In fact, what he did was pack everything into a bowling bag and return as quickly as possible to Los Angeles.

Once back in Los Angeles, Charley was afraid to get too deeply involved in drug dealing anymore. He thought that the people back in Phoenix had friends in

L. A. and would eventually get him for "burning them." This means cheating them out of their money. And he probably was right. He did, however, get lost in the city and refrained from drug dealing for the time being.

Naturally, Charley didn't refrain from using drugs himself. He was able to buy enough amphetamines to keep him reasonably happy most of the time.

Amphetamines were not that expensive, and he was able to get a job in a factory doing some lathe operating. He had learned this in the California Youth Authority facility. All of this time in reform school was not wasted after all. The lathe operation activity was fairly well paying. He was able to pay his rent and buy some new clothes. He even got a car to replace the broken down one he had driven from Arizona. Later on, he had enough money to buy some more things he wanted, a pistol and a shotgun to defend himself.

Charley was constantly afraid that the people in Phoenix were going to get him. Over the next several years, he actually became obsessed with this. Charley didn't get into very much trouble with the law for a while because he was working "fairly steady," and he had enough easily obtained amphetamines ("speed") to keep him happy. This was probably the most placid time in his life. But, of course, he kept taking the amphetamines daily. The erosion of his cerebral tissue continued with each dose. Finally, when he was about twenty-six years old, enough of the damage had been done so that his delusions and fears increased greatly. He began to feel that he was being followed by "the mob." He was certain that they were observing him daily and setting him up to be killed. He saw strange people following him at night in shadows which would fall across his path. He was terrified. He would drive along a city street and notice that a gray Chevrolet was behind him and then see that it changed into a brown Ford. This was clear evidence to him that "the mob" was chasing and following him and going to the great extremes of changing cars in order to throw him off the scent. Why they didn't actually kill him wasn't clear to him. But he knew it was just a matter of time before he was doomed.

On one occasion he became so terrified because he felt that someone was physically following him that he escaped from them by climbing onto a roof of a house in a suburb of Los Angeles. He then actually escaped by climbing on the other side of the roof, dropping down into some backyards and leaping over fences until the perceived pursuers were lost. The fact that no one else ever saw any of these pursuers did not change anything. He knew they were real and were out to get him.

On another occasion he was in a shopping center and knew that a car was following him. He cleverly drove his car to the edge of the shopping center and then went behind one of the stores and, again, climbed on the roof of the shopping center. He ran across the roofs of all the various buildings in the shopping center, getting to the other side before the mobsters could find him. On that occasion he went to the police and told them that he was being followed and that he was being shot at.

Unfortunately, the police didn't pay any attention to him and told him that it must be his imagination. They checked him for alcohol but, of course, he wasn't drunk. He doesn't know if they checked him for amphetamine use, but it is probably unlikely since no record remains of it, if it were done.

Charley's fears grew more and more lurid and terrifying as time went on.

He continued to work and show up for his job with the help of the amphetamines, and he continued to become more and more frightened. He armed himself with knives and ice picks. He got a better shotgun with more range that had an automatic pump. He became certain that he had to defend himself and that his days were numbered. He knew that he was doomed.

Finally, at the age of twenty-seven, he realized that his number was up.

Once and for all, he understood that he had to go to Phoenix and face "the mob." He decided to arm himself sufficiently so that he would be able to go there and wipe out all of his tormentors at one time. He prepared himself by loading up his car with ammunition and his reliable pump-action shotgun. He decided that the best thing to do would be to leave Los Angeles late in the day so that he would be able to arrive in Phoenix in the wee hours of the morning. That way, he would be able to strike at those who were pressing him when they were least ready for him. He also decided that the safest thing to do so that he could stay awake during his drive to Arizona through the night (and also during the battle that was going to ensue when he arrived there) was to take a lot of amphetamines with him. He obtained a whole bottle of "white crosses." This is the street name for pills called Benzedrine. Benzedrine has long since been out of use by physicians, but is a preferred drug by many "speed freaks." Charley, by this time, was a dyed-in-the-wool "speed freak." He lived for speed and, as we will see, he died for it.

Unfortunately, a lot of other people died for it too.

In order to prepare himself adequately for the drive, Charley took six or seven "white crosses" before he left. He wasn't sure, when the story was told to me later, how many he took altogether during that evening. But most of the bottle was gone when he was taken into custody by the Highway Patrol.

After leaving Los Angeles and swallowing at least eight to sixteen "white crosses," he was very alert. He began to note that probably the forces that were arrayed against him were greater than those that could be accounted for by simply some "gangsters" in Arizona. He then knew that his mission in life was a much more cosmic one. It had been his lot to be chosen by some unknown power to protect our planet from invasion by alien creatures. He became aware, as it begun to get dark, that aliens had in fact invaded the earth. They were probably Martians because he noticed as they drove by on the freeway that their faces had a green tinted appearance to them. The fact that the dashboard lights on many cars threw a green light didn't occur to him at that time, and later when we discussed it, he still didn't entirely believe that this was the case. The fact was that he was certain they were alien monsters who were disguised as human beings invading the planet.

Since he had armed himself with his shotgun, Charley knew that the fates had prepared him to be the defender of humankind against these things. He quickly determined his course of action. He knew that while driving along, if he opened the window on the passenger side of his two-door car, he could place his long-barreled shotgun on the window ledge itself. Then, if he drew even with the car containing the Martian monsters and got close enough to them, he would be able to wipe them out. He also realized that if the window were closed on the driver's side of the Martian vehicle, his blast would be less effective. Not wishing to waste ammunition, he knew that he could only strike at those Martians who had the poor judgment to leave their driver's side window open.

With this battle plan in mind, he stopped for a few minutes at the Banning, California, rest site to prepare himself. He loaded the shotgun and tested out his theory about resting it in the window. It was fine. He then set out to do battle. He drove along as dusk fell, and he could clearly see the green faces of the Martians. He came up alongside of a late model Pontiac and saw two monsters cleverly disguised as a middle-aged man and woman. They had made the mistake of leaving their window open. He drew up alongside of them and liquidated the first Martian couple. He knew he got the male driver, and he was fairly certain he also had hit the other Martian too. He couldn't stop to check it out, because his mission was too vital for that.

Charley proceeded on. He saw several other Martians who had left their windows closed, probably cleverly anticipating his attack. They didn't strike at him, so he moved on, accelerating until he got into the Coachella Valley in the Palm Springs area. There he noticed a great infestation of Martians, and began firing frequently. He later recalled that he must have wiped out at least a dozen or more alien vehicles.

By the time he left the Coachella Valley and was heading toward Blythe, he began to run low on ammunition. Also, he realized that he was almost running out of the Benzedrine tablets which he needed to keep his brain working well and to battle the green-skinned creatures. He decided that it was probably time to inform authorities of the invasion, and he started looking for a Highway Patrol vehicle to assist him.

He realized how fortunate he was as dawn came up when he saw the road block in front of him. He stopped his car in plenty of time, and got out of the car to run over and tell the officers how glad he was to see them and what had been going on. He was surprised when they arrested and handcuffed him, because really all he had been doing was trying to save humanity from annihilation.

When I interviewed Charley later in the county jail, he had been without his Benzedrine for two days. He was, in some ways, less bizarre, but still clung to the belief that he had only been doing a service for the rest of humanity and was greatly misunderstood. A great injustice was being done to him, and he wanted to tell me his story so that his rights could be maintained.

Psychological testing was obtained, and Charley cooperated in this too. The psychologist was of the opinion that Charley had a psychosis. He felt that Charley showed very definite signs of schizophrenia and, of course, that the schizophrenic manifestations had a distinctly paranoid flavor. This was, of course, due to his seeing monsters and Martians and alien creatures on many of the tests, including the Rorschach test and the other projective tests. Those are the kind where a person looks at either ink blots or ill-defined specific pictures of people doing things, and is asked to tell about them. He told stories of people harming each other, about invaders and monsters, and other frightening things. There was also the suggestion in the psychological testing of some organic brain damage. This, as you can imagine, is not surprising in the light of his long-term use and abuse of controlled drugs, specifically, amphetamines and stimulants.

Several other psychiatrists and psychologists also examined Charley, and the issue finally was joined in his trial.

The district attorney, after having seen the reports of three defense psychologists and three court-appointed psychologists and psychiatrists, finally obtained expert testimony from a physician from Northern California. This was a man who was not in fact board certified in psychiatry, but had been treating a number of psychiatric patients over the years. He took the position that nobody was able to claim immunity from the liability of his crime because of psychiatric illness. He felt that everyone was responsible for everything they ever did and, therefore, Charley was not able to maintain a plea of not guilty by reason of insanity.

In the ensuing trial, despite the testimony of all the doctors and psychologists that Charley suffered from a major psychiatric illness, the jury believed the physician who said he was responsible. It is hard to argue with that kind of choice since there were six people who were dead as the result of Charley's actions. There were a lot of other people injured and a lot of families who had suffered greatly. They decided that Charley should be held accountable, and he wound up getting six consecutive life sentences in state prison.

Charley had automatic appeals, of course, to these convictions, none of which were upheld. He went to state prison where he was unable to obtain the drugs of choice which he had used over his lifetime before this. He was, as we understand it from reports, miserable and unhappy, confused and agitated much of the time. His agitation and his confusion ended, however, after three years in state prison. He managed to obtain enough thin towels from the prison laundry to fashion a noose. He tied it to the top bar of his cell and strangled himself to death by hanging alone in the prison cell.

He never did succeed in defeating the Martians. The Martians may have succeeded in destroying him. More likely, though, it was the amphetamines and the stimulants that destroyed his brain.

This kind of bizarre, wanton series of crimes is usually explained by virtue of understanding how a human brain is physically destroyed. It is usually not due to the intricacies of an emotional conflict, the pressures of greed or lust, or other drives with which we are all familiar. This kind of individual is obviously greatly distorted and bizarre. The explanation for his behavior is not within the usual experience of each of us as ordinary people. Probably we have all had some experience with somebody who has had trouble reading or somebody who isn't a good learner, or somebody who has behavioral problems in school. All of these are certainly not dyslexic. All of these do not have organic brain syndromes.

Everybody who uses amphetamines does not have his brain destroyed. Everyone who grows up in a home in which the parents are either absent or unconcerned does not wind-up killing people wantonly on a highway. All of these factors however, brought together can, and frequently do, cause grief and destruction and, in this case and others, wanton homicide.

Charley's case is not unheard of nor, unfortunately, is it unique. The effects of stimulant drugs can be more than "recreational." In this instance, what we have actually seen come to pass is a gross paranoid psychosis. That is, the effects of these stimulant medications acted in this man's brain to such a degree that they robbed him of his ability to think reasonably and clearly and, in fact, began to encourage distorted and frightening notions in his thinking. Everyone from time to time is afraid of things. Everyone from time to time imagines that something may be happening which, when tested by facts, has not occurred.
In this instance, the frightening thoughts became overwhelming. The continued use of amphetamines encouraged the paranoid thinking and made the thoughts real.

The ideas became reality, and the ability to distinguish between fantasy and reality was lost. This is the essence of a psychosis, and in fact is how it is defined. A person who no longer is able to see the difference between what is real and what he imagines begins to think that his thoughts are actually coming to pass.

This man started as a child by having difficulties with his central nervous system. That is probably why he was troubled from the outset. He found that using stimulants made him feel better and, of course, like so many other people, if a little bit is good, then a lot is better. In his case, a lot was enough to cause total destruction of his thinking and eventually the destruction of other people. It even led finally to his own self-destruction, as we have seen. In this case of wanton and multiple murders, the motivation was in the fantasy of the killer. The fear and anxiety which he had had all of his life became real. And he acted upon his fears in a totally destructive fashion.

All of these murders did occur, and they all happened in a relatively small geographic area. They were generally in the Coachella Valley of California, which is essentially Palm Springs and the other desert resort communities. In fact, murder did occur in Paradise and, in this instance, it was a massacre.

The bright red thread of murder showed itself in Charley's case to arise from total and obvious madness. The insanity was, it might be argued, self- inflicted. That is, Charley never had to take amphet-amines or other drugs in the first place, and yet was it his fault that he had the problems that he did? Was it his fault that he was brought up in the way he was? Did he, in fact, fate himself to having a disordered and bizarre childhood? Wasn't he as much a victim as those drivers on Highway 10?

It could be argued that Charley's motive in the killings was to save the world from aliens. That was the argument that he gave to the police. But maybe all of us are to blame for not getting ahold of people like Charley sooner. Maybe there has to be more forceful interventions in deserved families and with children who clearly need help from the outside. These arguments in this particular case are moot.

Charley is dead and so are his victims. But there are other poten-tial victims out there. They are driving the highways right now. They may not always be in Palm Springs or even in California. There are lots of young men and women who are using amphetamines and "speed" and "coke." They, too, may start to see alien invaders sitting behind the wheels of cars. I know that I, for one, whenever I am driving along Route 10 at night always keep my window rolled up.

This is the first case for … A NEW WORD FOR MURDER

CHAPTER 2

The Kiss of Death

As we noted before, it is rare that the victims of a murder are unknown to the killer. Most of the time, the victim is his wife or her husband, or the business partner, or the good friend next door. The question is why doesn't the wife or the husband or the partner or the friend know that the other one has lethal plans for them? Sometimes the lust for murder is well hidden. Often, however, it is obvious that we just don't see it in time. If there is a core of madness inside of someone, there often are clues. The person close to the potential killer probably has many premonitions and many warnings, but chooses not to heed them. If we could interview the lifeless victims of many crimes, we would probably be able to elicit a great deal of information concerning how they could see what was coming, but chose to ignore it. We know that on occasion when a crime goes wrong, the victim then has lots of information about how they should have said this or done that and "should have known" what was about to happen. Even in the closest relationship between husband and wife and in their most intimate moments of love, the potential for death is near.

All of us who have studied Shakespeare in high school or college remember his famous play Othello. In it, the Moorish general winds up the play by murdering his wife, Desdemona, by strangling her while kissing her. This has been referred to in literature as the "Kiss of Death." Palm Springs police were confronted with a similar situation one night in April several years ago. They responded to a call by a distraught woman who indicated that her cousin had been murdered by her husband, both of whom were tourists visiting the "Golf Capitol of the World."

When they arrived on the scene, Henry Williams was sitting in the living room of a rented motel bungalow, and his wife's lifeless body was lying in the bed inside. There were purplish marks on her throat which fitted with thumb imprints of her husband. She had been dead and cold for some time, and Henry was staring mutely at the floor, softly sobbing. His wife, Joanne, was lying under the sheets naked, and Henry, it later turned out, had had intercourse with her, according to the coroner, very shortly before her death. Apparently, the crime had been committed just at the time that Henry was completing "the act of love" with his wife of twelve years. At the time of the murder, he was thirty-five and she, thirty-seven. They had been together for twelve years. They had lived together initially for five, and formally had married for the last seven. They had decided to take a trip to California from their native Wisconsin in order to take advantage of the warm climate. They could also visit Joanne's cousin, Kim, who lived there and worked as a waitress in a local restaurant. Kim had returned to the bungalow after work to visit Henry and Joanne for a drink before she went back to her own apartment after a night's work. When she arrived, she saw the same scene that the police observed upon their arrival. She was "so scared of what I saw" that, in fear of her own life, she fled from the bungalow to the nearest telephone, where she summoned the police.

Kim later indicated that she knew nothing of any arguments or problems between the couple, and thought that they were happily married. Although childless, they seemed to enjoy their lives together. Henry was a civil service employee with the city of Milwaukee, and had a responsible job working as a clerical person in the Parks Department. He seemed to be happy with his job and, as far as she knew, had never had any trouble with the law in the past.

Kim didn't know all of the facts. Upon Henry's arrest and fingerprinting, a computer check with the FBI was run. It appeared, that Henry had had some problems before. He had been arrested as a child for being a peeping Tom on several occasions. On one occasion, as an adolescent, he had been apprehended in a women's clothing store after having broken in. When found in the clothing store, the seventeen-year-old Henry had taken a knife to several thousand dollars worth of dresses and ripped them to shreds. This resulted in his being hospitalized at a juvenile facility in Wisconsin for more than a year.

Later, after his release, he began attending college in a nearby community.

While in college, he had been arrested for assaulting three co-eds with a table lamp in their apartment. Apparently, he had been invited to spend the night in the apartment with the three young women after a drinking party. During the night, Henry awoke and began attacking the three young women, using the table lamp as a club. This had resulted in still another arrest and a sentence of three years in a state institution for the criminally insane. Upon his release, he was placed on probation, completed college, and eventually got a job with the city.

The California court was concerned about his psychiatric history after the Palm Springs murder and, of course, the revelation of his previous activities.

Several psychiatrists and psychologists were appointed to examine him. It turned out that Henry had in fact been raised in a lower middle-class family in suburban Milwaukee. He had been the eldest of three children, and had been given what his parents had described as "a good religious education." They were fundamentalist Christians, and had believed in Sunday School, church-going and following the dictates of the Bible.

Henry's mother and father had their own room. They had never demonstrated any sexual activity in front of the children. Neither did they ever demonstrate any violence, arguments or fighting between themselves. They were strict but fair, in their view, and he confirmed this.

Henry recalled that when he was "a kid, maybe nine or ten," he used to get aroused sexually when he would fondle or touch his mother's clothing. He used to especially enjoy touching her shoes and under clothing. He soon began, however, to "cut, tear and twist the shoes and underwear." He recalled that while he didn't have sexual orgasms when he performed these acts, he did experience erections and felt great pleasure in his genitals during the cutting and tearing. The twisting and destruction of the clothing made him feel comfortable and warm. Later, when he did reach adolescence, he experienced orgasm during the violent ripping and tearing of clothing. This particular kind of activity continued throughout his life. He began to have sexual fantasies of cutting and tearing, not just clothes, but strangling and maiming women in connection with sexual arousal. He says that the beginning of this sexual excitement was about at the age of twelve when his parents, for some reason which he never did understand, actually separated. He was then raised exclusively by his mother.

He said that he always felt comfortable with his mother and never had any conscious feelings of anger or rage toward her. In all of the psychiatric evaluations this fact was mentioned and, to some extent, it was the feeling of many of the examiners that his very denial of anger or rage toward her was, in some way, significant.

As Shakespeare said in one passage, "Why so great a no?" In fact, it is the experience of many psychiatric and psychological examiners that when a person begins to deny things pointedly and vehemently, one has to look beyond the denial to see why it is so important to make that point. It became the suggestion of several of the examiners, including the present one, that this particular denial indicated that there very likely was a good deal of anger and rage directed against his mother. For reasons which are not clear and never became clear to Henry Williams, the rage never emerged directly against her. He knew that he always had feelings of positive enjoyment upon destroying and ripping his mother's things, especially her personal clothing. This probably was significant in his later behavior.

Henry did well in school and was a relatively bright young man. Even when he was involved in the destructive cutting and tearing of his mother's clothing and shoes, she never believed that there was anything especially abnormal nor problematic about this. She never imagined that psychiatric evaluation or consultation was in order. She regarded it as "a quirk" in his behavior, and let it go at that. He never attacked her physically nor anyone else in the family. Later, when he had his first encounter with the law, she was shocked and dismayed but, of course, supported him emotionally, and felt that he would "grow out of it."

In point of fact, Henry had his mind filled with sado-masochistic fantasies all through his youth, puberty and adolescence, to say nothing of his adult life. He would be fascinated by movies in which he saw women being attacked and assaulted. He would even have sexual arousal in horror films when the female victim would be apprehended by the monster or the mad scientist. Scenes in which she would be tied down to an operating table or trapped in a room awaiting the advances of the fiend who was to attack her or the monster who was going to dismember her would arouse him enormously. The notion of a helpless young woman being threatened by an attacker caused arousal, erection and, with a little manipulation, orgasm.

Henry later began to frequent neighborhood magazine and book stores so he could look at the covers of detective magazines. Usually these showed women being attacked, bound and gagged, and violated by criminals. He was terribly embarrassed about revealing this to anyone, and actually discussed it with no one. He felt that he was probably the only person in the world to have these kinds of sexual fantasies and these kinds of unusual sexual interests, and felt so ashamed of them he could never reveal them to anyone.

He experienced tremendous obsessional drives to obtain items of women's clothing and destroy them. This, of course, took the place of obtaining women's bodies and destroying them until later on in his life. He never really had ordinary heterosexual fantasies. That is, he never experienced any arousal at the sight of attractive girls. He was not interested in attending school functions or dances. He was not turned on by seeing cheerleaders jump around and contort their bodies at football or basketball games. He never, in the book stores, looked at "girlie magazines," but only at detective magazines. He was not especially interested in films, such as those with Marilyn Monroe, Rita Hayworth or other "sex queens" of his youth and adolescence.

He viewed sexual arousal and interest as something that one should keep quiet about and which one should treat with secrecy and shame. The sex act itself was murky and mysterious to him. He really wasn't entirely sure how it worked.

He was always afraid to ask anyone. Most of his friends would talk about dating and "scoring" with girls. He thought that meant having an orgasm in a way that was similar to the way he experienced orgastic pleasure while looking at pictures of helpless and violated women. He rarely, if ever, made the connection between their experiences of sexual intercourse and his own.

Later, when he finally went to college, he had read enough material to understand what an ordinary act of sexual intercourse was like. But he really had no major desire to engage in it. Apparently, he was regarded as being "safe" by the co-eds. Afterall, he never made advances towards girls whom he dated. He, in fact, only dated in order to keep up appearances and to appear to be the same as the other boys. He was very concerned about his past record and history of trouble so, generally speaking, always tried to be "good" and "normal."

Because he was bright and an active and energetic student, he did well in school. Henry was able to get scholarships and carry on in classes even though his mother was now alone and separated and unable to help him financially.

The event which culminated in the assault on the girls in the apartment was recalled by him later in a rather murky and dream-like state. He admitted that on the evening in question he had been at their party and had been drinking alcohol. He was not used to drinking alcohol, and felt that it fogged his thinking.

Eventually, he drank enough to cause him to get drowsy, and he started to fall asleep.

The next thing he knew he was awake and still somewhat intoxicated.

Apparently, the alcohol had dissolved his ordinary and usual inhibitions against acting out his violent sexual fantasies with real girls. On this occasion, he felt over whelmed with sexual desire. Upon seeing the three "helpless and innocent" young women sleeping in their apartment after the party, he felt unable to prevent himself from attacking them. His idea of attacking them was not to rape or violate them sexually but, essentially, to batter them with a blunt instrument. He became aroused even before he started hitting them.

It was, of course, during his attack on the girls that they awoke and began screaming. Their screams aroused neighbors, and the police were summoned.

Planning in advance was never one of Henry's strong suits.

During his entire three years at the state institution, where he was sent after the assault, he denied having rage against women, being angry with his mother or any other female. He saw the attack as the product of drinking. He never was able to fully understand the psychological implications of his sexual violence or urges. And, as before, he was so embarrassed, ashamed and overwhelmed with anxiety and agitation about these events that he could not deal with them, even with the psychologists who were assigned to help him at the state hospital. Finally, after his three-year sentence had been completed, he was released and promised himself never again to get into that kind of trouble.

Henry had met a young woman who worked as an aide at the state hospital in the female section, and became friendly with her. After his discharge, she, knowing about his background, was willing to date him and to see him. She, too, felt that his problems were related to drinking and that as long as he was able to stay sober, he would never harm her. In fact, through the entire twelve years of their relationship, he did not attack her in any way. He never, in fact, even shouted at her.

She was never aware of his sexual fantasies nor that he would continue to visit book shops and magazine stands to continue his interest in the covers and inside contents of detective magazines. She thought he was interested in detectives and police work, and she didn't think it unusual that he brought home so many of these lurid magazines. She never told her cousin nor her relatives about this, thinking that this was just an ordinary preoccupation of a man who had in fact been in trouble in his youth and was trying to "go straight" now.

He did, of course, masturbate frequently and openly during the period of their marriage. Again, his wife saw this as being in part due to the fact that he had great sexual appetites, and never knew that his masturbatory fantasies were surrounded by thoughts of violence, destruction and even death. She never dreamed that she was the target of most of them. They had ordinary and normal sexual activity during the course of their marriage, and this particular kind of activity would occur once or twice a week without anything unusual happening. The fact that during the intercourse he had fantasies of strangling, choking, stabbing and ripping her apart never was revealed to her until the deed was done. Even then, she probably died surprised.

Henry continued to scrupulously avoid excessive use of alcohol. However, after some time, he began to feel that he was safe, and he would drink on social occasions with his wife, under controlled circumstances. It was after those occasions that he recalled getting light-headed and sometimes thinking even more intensely about his sado-masochistic fantasies. But, generally speaking, he felt that they were under control and that he would never act them out again. As far as he can recall, he never did in fact tear his wife's clothing nor rip up her shoes, and certainly never broke into department stores or clothing stores to act out his fantasies during his adult life.

His job with the city was going well. He was accepted as a legitimate member of society after his previous trouble, and was in fact leading a normal and ordinary middle-class life. The fact that they didn't have any children was not surprising to him since his wife had been married before. She was somewhat older than he, and had not had children in her previous marriage. He felt this probably was just as well.

They were both able to work and made a good living, and had a good life style. They were able to afford vacations, and would go away from time to time, to Chicago and Miami, and once to New York City.

One cold winter day, several weeks before her death, Joanne informed her husband that her cousin, Kim, was working in Palm Springs. Since the weather would still be chilly in Wisconsin, it might be a good idea to visit Kim for the Easter vacation and enjoy the warm sunshine sure to be there in April.

Henry agreed that this was a good notion. It was then that fantasies started to work overtime. He began to think of how exciting it would be to murder and dismember both his wife and her cousin at the same time. The fantasies began to possess him, as he could visualize Joanne choking and gagging on her own tongue.

He saw Kim pleading for mercy as she watched him slowly kill his wife. Then it would be her turn....

He became frightened of these strong pictures in his mind, but again, never told anyone about them, and proceeded with their plans to take their holiday trip.

When they got to Palm Springs and came to the motel where they had booked their vacation, he felt that he would in fact be able to control the fantasies. Even having a few drinks wouldn't hurt him.

On the night of the murder, he did in fact have more than a few drinks. By the time he had four or five, he began to become sexually aroused by his now expanded fantasy. His wife, thinking that this was a signal of his interest in her sexual charms, became interested, and took off all of her clothing, and climbed into bed. She asked him if he would like to make love to her.

Henry saw her naked, alone and helpless in the bed, and thought this was his golden opportunity to act. He felt overwhelmed by the need to destroy her. Later, when Kim returned, he would kill her as well. He felt that being away from home somehow gave him license to do this. He was unknown in California. He was no longer the middle-class citizen of Wisconsin and the respected civil servant. He was now the fiendish, sadistic killer that he had seen in films and books thousands of times and relived in his fantasies on at least a million occasions.

With this fantasy in mind, he was able to become sexually aroused, and began having intercourse with his wife. At the time of his orgasm, he was possessed with the notion of killing her, and actually began strangling her as the orgasm proceeded. He recalled her startled look as he strangled her, and recounted that he lost track of how long he actually continued the strangling, only stopping when he realized that she had stopped making gurgling noises and that her face and lips had turned a purplish blue. He then realized, of course, that she was quite dead and even cold. He began dressing, and was fully clothed by the time the cousin returned.

He was by now overwhelmed with the enormity of what he had done. He was sober too. The fantasies which he had had for the past twenty-five years at last had come to fruition. He had actually killed a human being. It was no longer some clothing that he had torn or even some girl that he had injured. He was looking at a dead human being. The body was lying in the bed cold and unseeing. He was over-whelmed with remorse and grief. All of his sexual desires had been drained out of him, and he had indeed sobered up. He was no longer even interested in the cousin, whether it to be for sexual interest or even to acknowledge her presence.

He vaguely recalled her walking in and speaking to him. He had no idea what she said. When she went into the other room and saw her cousin's lifeless body and screamed and shrieked, he barely heard the noise. He vaguely realized that she had left, and some part of his mind told him that she was probably going to summon the police. He sat there until they arrived, sobs and tears coming from his throat and eyes. He knew that he had ruined his whole life and taken the life of the person who had been warmest and kindest to him.

When the time for trial came, he pleaded not guilty by reason of insanity.

He admitted that he had in fact murdered his wife, but said it was done in a period of loss of reason and, in some way, connected to his alcohol consumption.

The jury agreed with him and found him not guilty by reason of insanity. They also determined that he was a mentally disordered sex offender. He was remanded to the state hospital for the criminally insane for an indeterminate sentence, not less than twenty-five years and not more than life.

The newspapers were filled with descriptions of the murder and the "Kiss of Death." People followed the trial with great interest. A couple who had come to Palm Springs to enjoy the sunshine, to bathe in the pools, to play tennis or golf, had wound up in tragedy. One had died at the hands of the other, and the killer was going to spend the rest of his life in jail. Paradise had once again been violated by the mark of Cain.

The real core of this problem, of course, was the perverted sex-ual drive which had become confused in this man's mind with sadis-tic thoughts. Freudian theory teaches us that the two most import-ant instinctual drives that people have are those for reproduction and sexual activity plus those for survival and control of the environment. Sometimes the two get intertwined. That is, the drive for survival, which means physical endurance, strength and power in overcoming a hostile environment, gets sometimes mixed up with the drive for intercourse, reproduction and survival of the species. This often becomes seen by individuals as an interrelated activity. That is, sexual drive and the drive for control and power become merged.

The ultimate control, of course, of another person is to hold their life in your hands. Because this man never really had any reasonable understanding about sex and no sexual education at all, he was never able to talk to anyone about it. His view that he was the only person ever to experience this kind of intertwined feeling was at the core of his own destruction. Had he been able to talk to someone about this and to understand that this was a distortion of normal instincts, he might have been able to control it, divert it, or sublimate these drives in a more constructive direction.

Many people experience these kinds of feelings and are able to work them through. Many adolescents have these kinds of notions. The sale of thousands and thousands of detective magazines with lurid covers indicates that this is a subject which is familiar to as many men. Women, too, experience sexual fantasies of being raped and forced into sexual activity with some pleasure. Again, these are distortions of normal drives, and if understood can be handled in psychotherapy or even in counseling. It is rare that they are acted out in a violent and destructive manner. Even when the drives are very strong, they can be acted out in fantasy or play without causing violence or destruction to the partner of the opposite sex.

Sometimes strong fundamentalist religious prohibitions and rules can backfire. An individual who is never allowed to express his feelings or who believes that his feelings are evil, destructive and bizarre, never is willing to express them, and by hiding and burying them often causes them to emerge at other times.

The use of alcohol, which has been described by others as "the universal solvent," plays an important role in this. Alcohol is a solvent. It dissolves inhibitions and the normal pre inhibitions of civilized society. People frequently act out their fantasies while under the influence. Sometimes these fantasies are harmless and playful. Sometimes they are violent and destructive and cause the death and injury of others. In this case, the fatal combination was the dissolution of inhibitions by the alcohol and the presence of violent, hidden and terrifying fantasies in the killer.

While the particulars of this case are somewhat unusual, the events described did happen, are real and have happened before. an individual who becomes aware of a child who is in fact cutting cloth-ing, destroying pictures, acting in a violent and angry way towards members of the opposite sex should clearly pay attention to these signs and do something about them. Every young man who has these fanta-sies does not wind-up attacking co-eds or murdering his wife. Many of them, however, need help, and society owes it to the victims to see that they get it, or it could be another case for ...

A NEW WORD FOR MURDER

CHAPTER 3

Kill the Queer

The telltale crimson thread which we search for in each murder case sometimes begins early in the life of the eventual killer. It isn't the kind of thing that stands out clearly, and it isn't always discernible as a lethal flaw in anyone's life. Sometimes it turns out to be something that was noticed early on but always felt to be of minor importance or "something the kid will grow out of." Sometimes the drive to kill is not born in the child as an evil instinct, but arises almost accidentally as a defect in the fabric of that person's life. Sometimes it even seems that the later-to-be killer is just "unlucky."

Lady Luck was never very close to Paul Gould. Neither, were any other ladies. It wasn't that Paul did not like girls. He did. It was just that he had trouble being close to people, and most people realized this, he guessed.

Paul never had any special dislike for homosexuals or "queers," as he called them, either. He pointed out that after all he had grown up in a small, midwestern town where "that problem never came up. In Southern Indiana we didn't see 'those kind of people,'" he explained." We never had no trouble, and I didn't really think about it until later on."

Paul probably never had a lot of thoughts about many things. He had a lot of difficulty in his life starting as far back as we could trace. Records from his elementary school, which were later obtained by his attorney, indicated that he started to have trouble in the first and second grades.

By the time he was eight years old, it was pretty clear that he was what is now called "hyperactive." Some people have labeled this as a "minimal brain disorder" or "minimal brain dysfunction," but when Paul went to school he was termed by` his teachers and by his mother as "hyperactive," or just plain "hyper."

He was not able to sit still in class at all, and he had trouble with the teachers. He wanted always to talk to the other kids around him. He couldn't stay in one place. He would get up and move about. He was not able to really listen to the teachers, and finally he was sent to the school district's special psychologist for an evaluation.

The psychologist later sent him to the Child Guidance Center in Indianapolis, which was a big trip for his mother to take and "an awful lot of trouble." But they put him on some medication which she said did calm him down for a while. She was never really very happy about Paul having to take medication and also, of course, the trip to Indianapolis took more than an hour and a half each way, and was a big chore for her to handle.

She was having enough troubles as it was. Her husband, that is Paul's father, had finally left. They had been having trouble for years. The father, Paul Sr., was a violent man. He was easily angered, and things just never went right for him. As Paul's mother pointed out later on, "He just wasn't lucky."

Luck never seemed to be one of Paul Sr.'s assets. The jobs he got either went sour because the company went out of business or because the concepts grew so much that Paul was unable to cope with them; then he would be asked to leave. Or because Paul's chronic back problem flared up, he could not handle the physical work. "It was just one thing after another," pointed out the mother, Louise. Eventually, when Paul Sr. started to drink a little bit and maybe a little bit more, they started to fight. Paul Sr. had an explosive personality as it was.

When Paul Sr. drank it got worse. Louise sometimes would point out that he was drinking too much, and this made things even worse. Inevitably, on several occasions, he started to hit her, and she had to call in the sheriff. The couple were separated when Paul Jr. was eight and that is, of course, the same time he had to start going to the psychologist and then to the clinic in Indianapolis. Louise had to go out and get a job because Paul Sr. continued to have his bad luck and wasn't able to support the children.

It finally turned out that Paul Sr. left town and disappeared altogether. Louise, to this day, has not seen him since Paul was nine years old. "The sheriff looked for him for a while, and the district attorney, but they never found him. I don't know, some people just never do have any good luck. He meant well, but things never seemed to work out for him."

Louise, however, was an attractive woman, and she met another man and married him. He was pretty steady, and while he wasn't "exciting," he was gifted with a full-time job at Sears, Roebuck in their auto department. He was able to provide well for Louise and her two children and himself.

Things seemed to go a lot better for everyone, except of course Paul Jr. He still had his problems in school. The children in classes would tease him once in a while because he didn't seem to pay attention to a lot of things, and because they could get him to explode once in a while if they handled it right. That is, Paul Jr. would become angry and jump up and down sometimes when they said the right thing, and they thought this was "real funny." Paul Jr. remembers not thinking it was very funny at all. And he thought that the other kids were purposely trying to get "a rise out of me," and they succeeded. He tried unsuccessfully to control himself.

After the doctors in Indianapolis gave him the pills, he did feel much better.

He remembers he was able to do his school work pretty well, and while he did have some trouble reading, he was able to get by. He felt much calmer when he took the pills. Even though he sometimes got a little drowsy in class, it stopped his jumping around. He was able to pay attention, and he learned how to read reasonably well. He was always good at listening, and he understood what they told him in class all the time.

He got to be an average student. And he did not even mind going to Indianapolis once a month to see the people there. His mother, however, seemed to feel it was a problem. She really did not like the fact that he had to keep taking the pills. He remembers her talking to the doctor a lot of times and asking him, "Why does he have to keep taking these medicines?" The doctor seemed to think it was okay for Paul to take the medicine, and it really did seem to make him better all through school.

When Paul was twelve, however, the doctors seemed to agree with Louise's thinking and said they would try to get Paul by without any pills and see if maybe he just wouldn't "grow out of " his earlier problems.

Paul did learn how not to get teased too much and how to avoid talking all the time in class and how to not have the teachers look at him in a funny way. But he just could not get the knack of junior high school and of the complications of changing from class to class and having to do homework and paying attention to all kinds of things that he didn't like. While he, too, did not really want to keep taking pills forever, he did notice that he had a little more trouble concentrating when he didn't take the pills. Still, he was glad not to be on medicine and not to have to be a "freak," the way he had been before when he was going to the clinic and taking the pills.

From twelve to sixteen, Paul went to special schools in the county. While he was not in the regular classes with the other kids he grew up with, he was in with a lot of kids with whom he felt comfortable. They had problems the way he did in the past, and the special school was set up for them. They would still be able to learn things and not have to do so much homework. A lot of them were able to go out and get jobs and act more grown up than the other kids who had to go to that "sissy" high school.

Once in a while the kids would get into fights, but Paul felt he could handle himself. All he had to really do was to defend himself "a little bit." He didn't get the same kind of teasing in the special school that he had before from his so- called friends. So, he was happy, and even though he didn't learn as much, he finally was able to get out of school and get some kind of job.

His real goal was to join the Marine Corps. He had read a lot of good comics about the Marines, and he had seen all kinds of real good movies on television in which the Marines were doing all kinds of exciting things. He thought it would be a terrific thing for him to get into the Marine uniform and maybe some combat boots and go out to Vietnam and kill lots of Commies. That was his real goal in life, and when he was seventeen, he got Louise's permission to enlist early. His stepfather, of course, was glad to see him go and do his bit for his country, so they agreed. Paul joined the Marine Corps with their blessing and took a GED exam, and was able to pass it. He was a high school graduate and a Marine both at the same time.

He got along really well in the Marine Corps. He liked it there. He was seventeen, and he was building his body, and the Marine Corps was going to make him into a real man. He was happy in Camp Pendelton where he went for boot camp training. Later, when he was transferred to San Diego, he thought this was the greatest place in the world.

As he said, he really never had anything against queers, but they sure got him into trouble. He remembers that he was in this bar in San Diego and only having "a couple of drinks" with a friend of his when these couple of queers came in and started talking to him. Well, he knew what they really wanted from his life. They wanted to make him into a queer, and he wasn't going to let that happen.

Maybe he had a couple of drinks too many, he isn't sure, but he does know he got into a pretty big fight with them. The next thing he knew he was in jail in San Diego and was accused of having broken one of their jaws and jumping up and down on him.

They also said he had used a weapon. He doesn't remember any weapon, unless they meant the bottle he picked up when the guy tried to grab him. In any event, the charges were pretty serious, and the Marine Corps told him that civilian charges of that nature were "not consistent with the best interests of the service." He got a general discharge.

So that was one of his early experiences with homosexuals. He tried to avoid them after that if he could, because they had ruined his great career in the Marine Corps and maybe ruined his life.

After that, Paul went back to Indiana for a while, but never really liked it back there. He tried getting a job once in Chicago, and he even found a job with a truck driving company in Idaho. That did not work out either. He figured the best thing for him to do was to go back to Southern California because he liked it so much in San Diego.

Paul met a guy at the bus depot who told him there were jobs in Palm Springs. There are lots of jobs in Palm Springs in the winter because there were hotels that were open all year long but only really busy in the wintertime when the tourists came, at which time they needed extra help. Maybe he could catch on with a job there. If he did well, it could become a permanent career for him, and he could become a hotel man. That was something that wasn't as good as being a Marine, but it was going to be a living, and that is what he needed. So, he took the bus to Palm Springs and looked up a place that the man whom he met at the bus terminal told him about.

He got to this place. It was not the fanciest hotel in Palm Springs, he later pointed out, but "it was plenty good." It was one of the hotels in Palm Springs that had seen its better days. Like all resort communities, there is an emphasis on the newest and the best and the "in place" for the year. This place that Paul found, the "El Conquistador," had really been the "in place" sometime in the mid- sixties. It was the place where people would go to spend a week or two in the sun. Sometimes the movie stars who didn't have any friends who had weekend homes "in the Springs" would stop there too. Mostly, though, it was for the rich tourist who wanted to show off and come "to the Springs" for a long weekend or for a couple of weeks stay. Eventually, as time went on, the restaurant at the El Conquistador got to be fairly well known, and people began going there for gourmet food, at least until the newer places started to open up.

By the mid-seventies there were four or five other places that got to be more well known, that had a bigger dining room or a larger entrance hall, had a golf course on the premises, newer tennis courts, and the El Conquistador sort of slipped back to a middle level hotel. By the mid-eighties it was a little lower than that but still, as Paul could see, "a really good place to work." It needed a staff of some busboys and bellhops and general handymen, and Paul fit into all of these.

They were happy to give him a job there, and he worked hard so that he could become a success. He got to meet a lot of the customers, and while he recognized that many of them were "a little strange" and that they might be "queer as three-dollar bills," he knew that "you can't look a gift horse in the mouth."

What had happened, and this is not unusual in Palm Springs and similar communities, was that this became a hotel which had become the gathering place for homosexuals. A lot of homosexual individuals feel more comfortable with others who share their sexual preferences. It is not so much that they are looking for sexual activity per se, or even want to go "cruising" in their hotel. But they feel more comfortable knowing that they are wanted and accepted in a particular environment, and the El Conquistador had become known as "a safe place" to go in Palm Springs. Paul did not know this at first, but when he got there, he didn't really make much of it. The fact that he had had some trouble in San Diego he attributed to the fact that he had been drinking too much and that the people who came in had pushed him too far. He never really had any problems otherwise.

When he got to the El Conquistador, he knew that it would be all right there too. And it worked out that way. He never really had any major problems. Once or twice, some of the guests would wink at him or make a face at him, and he simply ignored them. He knew that if you didn't respond and make any gestures, they would simply leave you alone. He was told that by his friend, Harry, who had been working there for a long time and who wasn't queer either. Harry told him it was a good place to work, that the guys used to tip a lot and that they wouldn't push you unless you indicated that you were interested. The management did not want to have any "fraternization" between the help and the guests either. So, Paul felt pretty safe. He never really had any interest in gays otherwise anyway. He thought this would be a good place for him to learn the skills of the hotel business and to have a career.

Paul wrote to his mother back in Indiana that he had gotten a good job and things were going well. And they really were for several months. He got good tips, and he learned the business. He started to save a few dollars, and even hoped that he would be able to buy a car to get around California a little bit more and not have to be stuck at the hotel all the time, or have to take rides from people.

All of the gays had beautiful cars, he said, and he wanted to get one like theirs. "They had MG's and Porsches and all kinds of cars like that, and I thought maybe I could get one too." He was saving his money for this. "I kept my nose clean" most of the time.

Unfortunately, he did drink a little bit, but he felt that was okay. And once in a while he would get some marijuana from a friend and then he would smoke a joint now and then, but never got into any real trouble. He did notice that once in a while when he would drink or smoke grass, instead of it making him "mellowed out" like it did the other people, he would start to get a little more excited. And sometimes, "It made me paranoid." He noticed that when he smoked grass he would become suspicious and a little bit frightened once in a while. Paul thought that maybe someone was trying to take his money or trying to take advantage of him, and even once in a while put him down because he was "a hick from the country."

He got into one or two fights with some people, but nothing serious ever came of them, and he never picked up a bottle again or hit anybody with anything but his hands. So, there was no police record, and he wanted to be sure that didn't happen because he still a record from the troubles he had in San Diego.

He did very well the first season he was at the El Conquistador, and was promoted to becoming a bell captain. He was so good that management thought they would let him stay on during the summer when they let go a lot of the help. Many of the service people would go from Palm Springs during the summertime up north and work in the hotels at Lake Tahoe and other summer resort areas when the weather got really hot in the desert.

The El Conquistador, of course, was centrally air-conditioned. Management decided, with their skeleton staff, to stay open all summer long so they could maintain the place. Afterall, their clientele did come from San Francisco a lot and from other places to spend weekends. So, the place kept going with only a few guests during the week, and it was about half full on the weekends. This was okay with Paul, because it gave you a chance to relax a little bit, he thought, and make his plans work.

"It was really hot last summer, you remember that," he recalled, "and we had a few beer parties. I never got in any trouble in any of those parties. It was during one of the parties that all of this happened to me. Some of the guests used to hang around during the week with Harry and a few of his friends from town, and we had this party one night. There were lots of beer, and it was free. I didn't like to spend my money, so I went too. Harry thought I would have a good time.

We were just sitting around drinking beer when this guy came in with all this grass. He was one of those rich dudes from San Francisco. He was gay, I knew that, but I didn't think he was going to do anything to me. Everybody knew that I was straight. He had this really terrific car. It was a red MG. It didn't have a top. You could just jump into it from the outside without even opening the door, and drive it. It was probably the nicest one that had come down there that summer. He had all kinds of gold rings on his fingers and chains, and he was giving away the grass to all of us like it was made out of newspapers. He didn't care, and we had a terrific time. He was nice to me. But he didn't make any moves on me, and I thought that was okay, and maybe he just wanted to talk to me. I had an awful lot of beer, I think, I don't know for sure, and I had a few joints too."

"I was finally getting to the point where I was feeling really relaxed and so scared. It was pretty late at night, maybe three o'clock. This guy said to me that he was afraid he couldn't drive his car home because maybe he had had too much, and would I drive it for him. I thought this was a great chance to get to drive that car and see if I really like it, and maybe he'd give me a tip for doing the driving. Afterwards, I could walk home, it wasn't that far. So, I drove him back to his apartment. He had this place up in the hills. These queers have a lot of money, you know, and they don't mind spending it. This is really a fancy place up in "Little Tuscany.""

"Little Tuscany" is an area in Palm Springs which really represents the foothills of the San Jacinto Mountains. These are the large mountains which are west of Palm Springs and which create the environment which makes the desert community so geographically perfect. The San Jacinto Mountains are very high, and they face between Palm Springs and the coastal plain of California. Because of the height of the mountain range, it prevents many of the off-shore breezes and rain clouds from coming into the Coachella Valley and, in effect, creates the desert environment for which Palm Springs is known. It also, of course, creates the springs themselves. Since the rainfall which is dropped on top of the mountain never gets into the Coachella Valley beyond, it simply falls on the mountain range. The water then slowly seeps through the granite mountains to the underground water table and sometimes bubbles up in the form of springs in the valley below.

The Indians found this out hundreds and possibly thousands of years ago and began living in Palm Springs during the winter time. They would then move up into the foothills of the mountains in the summer. They had named the Coachella Valley in their own language, "The Palm of God's Hand," the valley, of course, being the actual palm of the hand and the fingers, which rise up from it, representing the mountains which surround the valley on all four sides.

It was to this little Tuscany condominium which Paul went, driving the possibly intoxicated man in his red MG. When they got there, Paul went inside hoping to get his tip. "The guy said to me that he had some really good grass, some Columbian stuff which he hadn't brought to the party and would I like to try some. I thought, why not? Nothing much was going to happen anyway, and I was okay, and I could use a little more grass anyway, and he was going to give it away. So, why not? I said, sure."

"He then said he would go inside and get some, and he brought back a little black box that was all shiny, and inside he had these joints already rolled, and said for me to help myself, that he was going to go inside and change into something more comfortable. He asked me why didn't I take off my shirt because it was really warm and the air-conditioning hadn't started to work yet. I thought this wasn't a bad idea. I really didn't know what he was up to, I guess. I'm not always able to think so clear when I'm drinking beer and smoking grass, so I took off my shirt and lit up a joint."

"It was really a fancy place. It had all kinds of pictures on the walls, little statues and really nice furniture. There were a lot of pillows and cushions and velvet stuff all over the place. I sort of laid down on this velvet cushiony kind of couch, and smoked my joint."

"Well, he came back about ten minutes later, and he really scared the shit out of me. He didn't have any clothes on at all. He was totally naked, and it looked like he had been rubbing himself with some kind of smelly oil. He was all sort of shiny and glistening, and he came out and kind of paraded himself around and said, 'Are you having a good time?' I guess I didn't answer him for a while, and he continued to say, 'Well, let's have even a better time,' and he sort of grabbed for me. I think I got scared and maybe I panicked."

"The next thing I knew I picked up one of these metal statues which was kind of gold in color and really heavy. When he came after me and tried to grab me again, I hit him with it. I guess I hit him pretty hard, because the first time I hit him he just sort of fell down. He fell like a rock. I don't think I hit him more than once, maybe I hit him twice, I'm not sure. It's hard to remember. I was kind of spaced out with all that beer and grass and whatever, but there was an awful lot of blood coming out of his head. It was really pouring out, and I must have freaked. I was really scared. I didn't know what to do. But I figured I had better get away from there. I figured I better take the keys to the car and get out. He had taken the keys when we got there and put them in this little sort of purse that he had, this little leather bag. I reached in there to get them. I took the keys, and there was some money there too. I figured I better make my getaway, and I had to get out of town, so I took the money too. There was maybe two hundred dollars. I took that and the keys."

"I got in the car and started to drive away. But I had so much panic in me and so much fear in me that I had trouble getting the car going, and I couldn't get it into the right gear. I was able to do it when I took him there, but this time I couldn't get it out of first, and I sort of drove down the hill in first gear. It started to make noises and smell kind of funny, and I just left the car there at the bottom of the hill. I didn't want to keep driving. It was making all that noise. I got out. It was only a few miles, and I ran back to the El Conquistador."

"When I got back to the hotel it was about four o'clock in the morning, and I went over to Harry's. Harry was asleep, I guess, by then. He had been kind of bombed out at the party too. But I woke him up, and I told him that I had to get out of town. He asked me what had happened, and I told him. I told him that this guy tried to attack me and tried to rape me, that I got scared and I think I hit him and I don't know what happened. I didn't think I killed him, but I knew I was in trouble. I told him I had a record in San Diego for hitting somebody before, that the best thing for me to do was to leave. I asked him if he would please get dressed and drive me to the freeway where I could hitch a ride. Maybe I could go to Phoenix or L. A., or someplace out of town before they found this guy."

"I figured Harry was my friend. He always said he was my friend, and he was the one who got me the job and kept telling me that things were okay, and I trusted him. He told me to just sit tight and he would see what he could do. He stalled around for a while, and I kind of thought he was afraid to take me. I asked him again, and when I came back, I had all my stuff packed in my bag, all the stuff I was going to take anyway. I still had the money, and I said if he couldn't take me, I was going to take a cab or something like that. I had to get out of town right away, and there were no busses that time of day. Harry said to wait just a few more minutes and he was going to be okay, he just had to get awake."

"Finally, we walked out in front of the El Conquistador, and there were all these cops there. There must have been ten of them. I never saw so many cops in that little town in my life, and they were all there at the same time in the early morning. I guess they must have waked up some of them because they were kind of mad and mean, and they pushed me around a little bit. They told me that the guy was dead, and I was under arrest for murder."

"Later, they told me that they had arrested me for stealing the car and the money, and they even said that they thought I had probably planned the whole thing ahead. They told me some detectives had talked to some of the people at the party and that I had said something about all his gold rings and his chains, and that I would really like to have them, and his car too. Maybe I said that, but I sure didn't mean it. I didn't mean to go and take it and rob him and kill him, and all that stuff. I guess I'm just unlucky, like my father. You know, my dad, he had a bad temper, too, and he used to get mad, and he hit my mother a few times. I remember that. Finally, he had to leave town. But she never got hurt real badly."

"I guess I'm just unlucky. If I had picked up something else, maybe a lamp or some other statue that wasn't so heavy, or maybe if I had just hit him myself with my hand, I wouldn't be in all this trouble. I don't know what to do now. I know I didn't mean to do it. I didn't mean to kill the queer. I just meant to keep him away from me. Do you think you can tell them that I didn't mean it, and that I won't do it anymore?"

Paul, according to California law, of course, was not able to plead insanity or not guilty by reason of insanity. He really can't be considered insane, and there was no way that his lawyer could invoke that defense. I was asked to see him to evaluate his mental status and whether or not he was competent to assist in his own defense. By legal standards, of course, he was.

The fact that he did have some mitigating circumstances, that is, his susceptibility to booze and to drugs is no excuse in the eyes of the law. The law takes the position that when you drink or use drugs, you are doing so on your own volition and your choices are your own. What those substances do to you and how they make you act becomes your own responsibility. So, Paul had no defense insofar as the drugs were concerned. The only issue was whether or not he had planned the crime, or whether it all happened in the way that he said. The district attorney took the position, of course, that it was all pre meditated and planned in advance. The public defender tried to convince the jury that it was a series of events which overwhelmed this young man and that while he obviously had killed the victim, he didn't do it with malice or forethought or premeditation, but mainly as one of the series of explosive episodes in his life.

The jury did, in fact, believe the public defender, and Paul was convicted of second-degree murder. He was sentenced to fifteen to twenty-five years in the state penitentiary. What this means in reality is that if he stays out of trouble and is a model prisoner, he will be eligible for parole in about seven or eight years.

Whether or not they give him parole is another question. With murder cases they often wait until the minimum sentence is served. That would be fifteen years before considering a parole.

The traditional psychoanalysts would say that Paul had a homosexual panic when he killed his victim. This means that they believe many young men are so afraid of sexual impulses towards other males that they can become terrified of the impulses being carried out. They then, theoretically, will panic. Under these circumstances, they can act bizarrely and unreasonably. Flight or fight are among their choices. Paul may have panicked and first fought. That is, in his terror of acting out a homosexual impulse, he struck out against the possible object of his lust. Then, in theory, still terrified, he fled.

While the actual truth probably lies somewhere in between more biochemically oriented psychiatrists would theorize that the reason why Paul committed the crime probably can be best understood by his volatile personality and his extreme sensitivity to drugs. Lots of people drink and a lot of people use drugs. Sometimes they use them together. Obviously, everybody does not go around bludgeoning people to death or panicking, or feeling that they are being attacked. They certainly do not defend themselves the way he did. But given his background and his family history, it is not surprising that these things happened.

Paul probably was always a hyperactive child. Today we have changed the description of that disorder to, A.D.D., Attention Deficit Disorder. What it really means is that there is some kind of trauma that was experienced in his birth or some kind of metabolic defect that was inherited from his family which causes him to be acutely sensitive to certain medications and substances. The defect also makes it very hard for these kids to focus and think clearly under ordinary circumstances. That is, the kids who are six or seven years old and who, in a class for the first time, cannot sit still and cannot keep quiet. They cannot pay attention and often are diagnosed as having this problem of hyperactivity. They have difficulty, really, in focusing their attention and in concentrating. They may not always be hyperactive, and that is why this term has now been dropped in the psychiatric literature. Sometimes they are hyperactive and run around and can't be contained in one place. Sometimes they just can't focus their attention, and what seems to be restless movement is really the roaming around of an individual who can't find one thing to focus on or to pay attention to.

In Paul's case, probably both were true. That is, he jumped around and moved about and could not sit still, and also could not pay attention nor easily learn.

When he was taken to the clinic in Indianapolis and given medication, which turned out to have been Ritalin, it helped him a lot. Ritalin is a drug that acts paradoxically in people with this disorder. That is, most people who take Ritalin find themselves stimulated, and it is used widely in elderly people to give them more energy and alertness. In young kids who have a disorder such as Paul's, that is, "Attention Deficit Disorder," or Hyperactivity, it works in the opposite manner. Ritalin causes them to calm down and to be relaxed and to actually be able to focus their attention.

It worked this way in Paul for four years, as far as we can tell from the records that we obtained. Because it is a drug controlled by the Federal government, it creates a problem for both the parents and the doctors. This is because the prescription has to be rewritten each month and renewed at a pharmacy without telephone renewals, and the like. This is, of course, in order to prevent its abuse by people who do not need it or who might use it really as a substitute for "speed" or amphetamines. Amphetamines do have the same effect on hyperactive children, and have been used for a long time, as well as Ritalin.

There are some other substances which are similar and which can be used effectively too.

In Paul's case, the medicine worked, but the mother got more and more restless with the problems of having to go to Indianapolis, to get the medication, and to keep him on it. She began to press the doctors to stop. A lot of people think that when somebody calms down and gets better on medication, the medication should be stopped. This is often true. Unfortunately, for a lot of people, though, the only reason they are better is because they are taking the medicine. When they stop, they get worse again. There is a kind of magical thinking on the part of a lot of patients that says, "I'm sick and I have to take the medicine." This is followed by, "I'm taking the medicine and, therefore, I'm sick." This kind of thinking then leads to "If I can just stop taking the medicine, I won't be sick anymore." This was Paul's mother's approach to the situation. Finally, she convinced the doctors when Paul Jr. was twelve to stop the medicine, and they took the position that "maybe he would grow out of it anyway," however, he didn't.

Most kids do not grow out of hyperactivity syndromes. What they do is learn how to adjust socially. They learn how to stop jumping around. They learn how to stop talking in class. Eventually, they learn how to conform their behaviors to the requirements of the institutions in which they find themselves. This does not really change their thinking patterns nor their susceptibility to medications or drugs, but it does make them appear to have "gotten better." They remain very susceptible to paradoxical effects of drugs, however. That is, while stimulants calm them down, sedatives make them excited.

If Paul had been in treatment all along, it could well have been that the blood red thread of murder might have faded over the years. The hair-triggered temper, the inability to control his feelings in any direction when they were intense, and the susceptibility to other drugs could all have been tempered with treatment and understanding. As it happened, however, there was no understanding, there was no treatment, and there was another death. Perhaps this was inevitable. Perhaps it is that we all have the crimson line of blood lust within us. Only some of us are luckier than others and able to control it. Paul wasn't that lucky, and his victim was even more unfortunate. Paul is in jail, his victim is dead, and we have another example of ...

A NEW WORD FOR MURDER

CHAPTER 4

Take the Money and Kill

Up until now some of the descriptions of the core of murder and the reasons for the killers doing what they did can seem alien. These were not normal people. These were bizarre and distorted people. One was crazy from the start.

Another was defective because of his hyperactivity, and still another was a "pervert." Most of us don't have to worry about that. We are never going to get to be in that position. We don't have to worry about our families and our kids being that way either. Afterall, we are "normal," aren't we?

One of the All-American boys suddenly turned to murder to solve his problems? Suppose Jack Armstrong or some other Astronaut were suddenly accused of a vicious, wanton and bizarre killing? How could it be understood? What could the reason possibly be? Why should anyone with that much going for him throw it all away? There usually are answers.

Tom Winters, from the outside, seemed to be a typical and wonderful American success story. Tom was a twenty-five-year-old boy from Southern California who had worked his way up on his own to become the chief executive officer and major stockholder in his own TV music company. He had his own company and all the things that went with it. All the trappings that success offers in our society were his. He had a condominium at a country club in Palm Springs. It was furnished by an interior decorator of some renown. He had a bright red German sports car and European suits that cost six and seven hundred dollars each. He had beautiful girls who seemed to be constantly attached to him, either staying at his condominium or meeting him in nearby Los Angeles, or calling him on the phone three or four times a day.

Tom was a good-looking young man. He was about six feet tall, and had rather dark, curly hair. He was not well built in the football player mold, but he had a wiry, athletic appearance. He looked as though he worked out every day, which of course he did. He played tennis at his condo and was fairly good, making it reasonably well in the B group.

All of this was probably unexpected to those who knew him earlier in his life. Tom was the eldest of four children born to George and Harriet Winters who lived in suburban Los Angeles. George had a job with the local milk company, and worked in the office there as a supervisor. He made an adequate income, but not enough to send his children away to college or to support them after graduating from high school. Tom was a bright young man and good looking, and knew that he had to make his own way if he expected to get anywhere in the world. And he certainly did.

He had always known that he did not want to be the mirror image of his father. He did not want to work for a milk company or a phone company or a cab company or a power company or, in fact, work for anyone. He wanted to be his own man and to do his own thing. He decided this early on in his life.

He graduated from high school with fairly good grades, but nothing startling. He managed to get accepted at one of the universities in Los Angeles. Because he was able to live at home and, at the same time, get some government loans, he made it for a couple of years in college.

While in college he needed some pocket money, and due to his great ambition and drive he managed to find peripheral work in the entertainment industry. At this time, Los Angeles is, if not the capitol of the entertainment industry, at least second only to New York in terms of the number of various enterprises which are based in Southern California. The movie business, the record business, the television business, and others are based in Los Angeles.

Tom got a job with a TV producing company. He started out as a gofer. A gofer is a term that has evolved over the years in that business, and it really started out probably in New York show business in the legitimate theater. The gofer was the young man who would go for coffee or sandwiches or cigarettes, or make a call or bring back a newspaper or, in some way, run around at the direction of the producer or director or star. Eventually, the term gofer became one in common use and, while most companies gave these young men titles, such as assistant associate editor or assistant junior director, or the like, everyone knew what it was that they did. They were the yes men and the runners and the toilers in the vineyards of show business, who hoped to make it big someday.

Tom recognized that this was a potential area for him to make it and to make it big. He decided to exploit that to the greatest extent he could. He was always one to keep his eye out for the "main chance." He felt that the record business or the movie business or the TV business offered a chance for a "big score." In this instance, while working for a company that made TV commercials and small films, he got an idea which seemed to take off. He saw the beginnings of using TV films to exploit records. These later have become known as TV videos, and have been on cable TV for the past several years. They are, in effect, visual portrayals of popular records and songs. Tom early on saw that these videos were going to be something that was in greater and greater demand, and thought that he might get in on the ground floor.

After working for two years for his boss in the commercial TV business, he managed to get ahold of some money (by borrowing it mainly) to set up a company to make TV videos. At the beginning, nobody really questioned where he borrowed the money from. Everyone knew that he did not have it himself.

They assumed he got it from people he met in his connections while working for the TV company. Possibly he got it from performers and possibly from other producers, or people who had cash. It is the kind of business where there is a lot of cash easily available. This probably also explains why it is the kind of business where dope and Cocaine and marijuana are easily obtainable and widely used.

Tom was not one, however, who used heroin or marijuana or Cocaine, or any other drug, as far as anyone knew. He always looked wholesome and healthy. He was always sober and cool and, in some people's minds, a little calculating.

Tom's business flourished quickly. The videos sold widely and money began to come in. He started to travel in faster and faster circles. He started to drive faster and faster cars. He began to hang out with faster and faster women.

Everything in his life accelerated. He began to spend money almost as fast as he made it. Maybe he felt he had to buy the condo in Palm Springs. It was the in thing to do. He knew that he had to buy the Italian suits and special shoes and even the silk underwear. You had to wear one-hundred-dollar shirts to be anybody!

He couldn't seem like a boob and not go to Vegas with the others either.

Sometimes, you had to pop for a few bucks and entertain your friends. So, what if he had to go on the tab once in a while at the casinos. He had a lot of friends after all, and he had to take care of them. So, what if he had to borrow money from some of the "wise guys" in Hollywood once in a while. There was more where that came from. You had to keep up appearances in show business, and the number of his friends and acquaintances and "business" associates grew, as they felt they had hitched their wagon to his star.

It might have been that things were not always going well for him because he had expanded so rapidly and so quickly. Maybe everything he made did not sell and everything he touched did not turn to gold. There was even some talk around the Springs that he was cash short. Things still looked good on the outside. The condo, the sports cars, the Italian suits, and the hot and cold blondes running in and out of the country club all spoke of an American success story.

This made it all the more incredible when Tom was arrested by local police and was charged with a year-old murder.

A year prior to the arrest, there was a story in the newspaper about a body being found in a destroyed car out on the U. S. Air Force bombing range near Palm Springs. The bombing range is an area of the desert which is quite isolated and inside of a large tract of government-held property which the Air Force has used for many years, dating back to World War II, as a bombing and testing range. Apparently, they paint big targets on the desert and drop bombs from airplanes, or set up things for fighters to strafe and shoot at, and the like. There are occasional announcements of war games going on up there and people stay clear for fear of getting even close to that kind of artillery and explosiveness.

On this occasion, however, it seems that there was an explosion when there were no scheduled war games and no flights or bombing runs logged. At first, it appeared that some poor soul had been out in the desert driving in a four- wheel drive truck and ran over an unexploded bomb. According to the newspapers, the body was blown to bits and identification was not easily possible. That was about the last anyone heard of that story.

When it appeared in the newspapers that Tom Winters was arrested and charged with the murder of a man named Eugene Field, there did not seem to be much connection. In point of fact, there was great wonderment locally as to what this had to do with anything. It was later announced, however, that Eugene Field was the identity of the dismembered and exploded body in the car found on the testing range.

The sheriff's deputies and the FBI had worked together on this since the body was found on Federal property. With the help of both the State of California Justice Department and the FBI, Mr. Field's remains revealed enough information with which to identify him.

Tom hired the best attorney he could find to defend him. There was some question about whether or not there was probable cause. There were also a lot of questions about the witnesses who were turning up to testify against him. It appeared that the state had found two witnesses who were willing and ready to swear that Tom Winters had, in cold blood and solely because of greed, murdered Mr. Eugene Field in their presence and with their assistance.

The general contention of the district attorney was that Tom's finances were not going as well as he wanted everyone to believe. He had become too deeply into debt, and through overexpansion was really not making enough to cover his debts. It also appeared that he owed a lot of money to some people who were not tolerant of his not paying promptly. They were the kind of people who were not interested in foreclosing, but who would collect their debts in a more forceful manner. The D.A. suggested that Tom borrowed the money initially from dope peddlers and pushers whom he met in Los Angeles and that these people were only interested in immediate returns of exorbitant interest, and he was falling further and further behind. There was the further suggestion that Tom, in order to meet the growing needs of his debt service, had himself become involved in some drug transactions.

Apparently, Mr. Eugene Field was a pilot who had been well known to the FBI and to the U.S. Border Patrol. He was an airplane pilot who flew between Southern California and Mexico hauling in large shipments of either marijuana or Cocaine, or whatever there was available for distribution and sale.

The government alleged that Tom had financed some of these sales.

Moreover, they said he was involved in setting up some others in order to take care of his overexpansion, his debt and, of course, to pay for his rather extravagant expenses and life style. They claimed that they intended to prove this. Tom, of course, denied both in court and publicly that he had any guilt whatsoever.

It was Tom's contention that he had never been involved in illegal drug activities, that he was just a young man who got sucked into some loans by some very bad people who were putting the pressure on him. He further said that he really didn't know anything about drug trafficking but that the loan sharks had begun to put pressure on him. Finally, when he was unable to come up with everything and refused to sign his record company over to them, they had framed him.

He said that while it was true, he knew Mr. Field, and Mr. Field had been a visitor to his house on many occasions, he only knew him because of his interest in airplanes and flying. He said that on the night in question when Mr. Field disappeared and later was apparently killed, Mr. Field had been to his house briefly after flying somewhere in Southern California. He had a few drinks and then left quite healthy and alive. He also pointed out that Mr. Field left in the company of two other men whom Tom had met through his business and who were only acquaintances. These two young men were about his age. One was a fellow named Aurelio Gomez, who was in some way associated with the music business. Tom had known him on and off over the years, and Gomez had visited him and played tennis with him on a few occasions. The other young man was named Jack Casey. Jack, he knew to be a mechanic, and apparently was a friend of Aurelio's.

He said that he had never entertained Jack in his home before, but that Aurelio had brought him over that night for a visit and that they had met once or twice before in connection with some interest that Jack had in his red sports car.

It was Tom's contention that both Aurelio and Jack were setting him up. It was probably because of some plot that the loan sharks had against him. Tom swore that he was free of any guilt, but that Aurelio may well have had something to do with the crime because he was "a speed freak" and was constantly "crazed out of his mind" on drugs. He didn't know, much about Jack except that he had heard that Jack had been in trouble with the law on one or two occasions in the past.

Tom had no record of any kind of criminal activity, and never even got in trouble at school. He was a model student and had model conduct. He had deported himself always as a gentleman and dressed properly. He spoke well, and it was the general opinion among his friends and acquaintances that it was at least possible that he was telling the truth. How could the district attorney and the state pick on a man like this without any substantiation or proof?

Insofar as Tom's psychological makeup is concerned, again, he sort of fits the picture of middle America. He had an intellectual capacity in the range of bright-normal. That is, he was around 115 to 120 in IQ. He had a good vocabulary, but not more than one would see in a college student. He had good social adaptability and verbal ability, and was able to do problem solving at reasonably accurate levels. He seemed to show some difficulty in testing under: pressure, and started to make errors when he was pressed. He got a bit irritable at times like that.

Despite this irritability, however, he quickly recovered and always said the socially correct thing. He backed away from becoming openly hostile and angry, although the examiner felt that he could detect, under the surface, a good deal of anger, impatience and distress. There was nothing especially unusual in his projective tests, that is, the Rorschach (the famous ink blot test) or other tests which were calculated to get some understanding of his unconscious thinking. Again, there were some suggestions of pressure causing anxiety and agitation, as well as some indications of his feeling a good deal of rage and anger, which were well contained under the smooth surface of his personality and its veneer. These were suggestions only, however. There was no indication that he was psychotic, out of touch with reality or in any way unable to understand what was going on, or to deal with the problems of life in an appropriate manner.

The general feeling was that while he was relatively adequate and normal appearing in psychological testing, he was not always completely forthcoming and certainly not as ingenuous as he appeared on the surface. It seemed that there was something a bit contrived about Tom. But there was no hard evidence to prove this either.

His background indicated that he grew up under some circumstances of control and rigidity. This was brought about by a rather controlled and rigid set of parents. They felt that their lives would be comfortable only if they knew every alternative that was being placed in front of them and if they handled everything that arose in the most conservative and safe manner. Tom felt that their consciousness of always playing things safe and their awareness of always doing things strictly "according to the rules" was their major flaw. It was his belief that his father had much more talent than his simple job at the dairy would allow him to perform. He felt that his mother was brighter than a housewife had to be. But she was afraid to take a chance and to do anything in her life. He felt that if he himself didn't "grab the bull by the horns," he would always remain stuck in a small, middle-class suburb. He had watched television, read magazines and had gone to the movies, and knew that there was a lot more in life for him than suburban, middle-class America.

He fantasied himself as a man about town. The culmination of his dreams was the condominium in Palm Springs and the red sports car and the starlets racing about. He had had it all within his grasp, and now someone was trying to take it away from him.

When Tom's case finally came to court, the story that the witness told seemed rather convincing. It was also very dramatic. Gomez testified that Tom was getting deeper and deeper into debt to the loan sharks and that they were pressuring him to become more involved directly in drug deals. They said that the only way he could pay back for the vast sums of money which he owed them was to "take some chances."

It appeared they needed a middleman to accept the drugs from their pilot and to carry them into the city. It was much too dangerous to fly drugs in directly to Los Angeles or to the surrounding airports. Palm Springs offered a useful alternative. The local airport could not be used all the time either, but there were even more remote places where one could land a plane and go undetected. If someone had a four-wheel drive vehicle, he could meet the plane, pick up the drugs and then transfer them to a red sports car in Palm Springs and drive to Los Angeles undetected to make the deliveries. This was to be Tom's role. Gomez was to be his assistant, or possibly gofer.

They carried out, according to Gomez, one or two of these drops and, in effect, they became "mules." "Mules" are individuals who carry things for drug traffickers. The term is used in a somewhat negative fashion because, of course, mules are felt not to have very good brain power and are being used by their masters only for their brawn and relative reliability. Tom greatly resented the role of being a "mule" and, according to Gomez, was constantly thinking of ways to "turn it around." It finally became clear to Gomez that what Tom had in mind, in terms of turning things around, was to go into business for himself. He would appropriate one of the major deliveries and tell the people to whom it was being directed that the pilot never arrived and that something must have happened to him. Maybe he crashed or got caught or "had an accident of some kind."

Gomez said that at the beginning he agreed to be part of the plan, not only because he, too, was greedy and wanted to get a bigger "piece of the pie," but because he was terrified of Tom. He said he had never met anyone with such force of will and who was so ruthless before. Gomez had been around in the gangs of Los Angeles and knew whereof he spoke. He said that he agreed to do what Tom wanted because if he didn't "Tom would get me too."

The usual plan was to accept the drug delivery from Eugene Field by driving Field's four-wheel drive vehicle from Tom's-house to a remote spot in the desert where Field would land. Field would then transfer the goods to the four-wheel drive vehicle. They would jointly drive it to Tom's condo where the transfer would again be made to the red sports car. Field would be paid off, and Tom would then deliver the material to his masters in Los Angeles. Instead of doing this, it was Tom's idea to simply appropriate the drugs and "get rid of Field." They could then drive the car back out to the desert and leave it there as if some accident had occurred, destroying both the drugs and Field at the same time.

According to the plan, Gomez and Tom were to go out at the appointed time and meet the plane. Jack Casey was contacted and convinced to meet them afterwards at Tom's condo. They felt that they needed Casey in order to carry out the plan to its fullest and most practical degree. Casey had been a demolitions expert during his service in the Vietnam war. It was Tom's idea to kill the pilot after taking the drugs and making sure they were intact. They would keep Field's payoff for themselves. Then they would drive the car back to the desert where they would blow it up and make it appear as though it had run over an undetonated bomb. For this purpose, of course, they needed Casey's services. He was promised a large portion of the profits and also, according to Casey and Gomez, Tom threatened that he would "take care of you too" if Casey didn't agree to the plan.

On the evening in question, Field arrived at a desolate airstrip in the "High Desert" of Southern California. The High Desert is simply an area of the western desert which is elevated somewhat higher than Palm Springs. It is three or four thousand feet from sea level. It is sprinkled with plateaus and flat places and very sparsely populated. It certainly makes an ideal place for the landing of airplanes when the pilot doesn't want others to know of his arrival.

They, according to Gomez, met Field and greeted him warmly. He had a good flight. He was undetected by the Border Patrol or anyone else, and felt that he had pulled off another coup. He had a large amount of marijuana, as was planned, and even some Cocaine which he had managed to obtain on his own. He demanded payment, and Tom told him he would give him the eighteen thousand dollars he had been promised for the flight upon delivering the stuff to Tom's condo in Palm Springs.

The three went off in the four-wheel drive vehicle to complete the transaction. When they arrived, Tom gave Gene Field his money, all in cash and in hundred-dollar bills. They then transferred the goods from the four-wheel drive vehicle to Tom's condo and put it in a locked storeroom where Tom would be able to take it into Los Angeles a bit at a time without detection. Tom invited Gene to have a drink with him and Gomez, and said that they would be joined by another friend in a little while. Gene said he didn't have time to wait, because he still had his Cocaine and didn't want to be walking around carrying it. So, if they didn't mind, he would just have a quick drink and leave:

Tom, realizing that he really could not wait for Casey to show up, asked Gomez to come with him downstairs "to check the lock," and told Gene Field that they would be right back. While downstairs, Tom told Gomez that they could not afford to waste any more time and that as soon as Field had the drink in his hand, Gomez was to grab him about the arms and hold him tight while he (Tom) knocked him out. Gomez claimed that as far as he knew, Tom's intention was only to knock out Field and to take off with the drugs. He said he didn't know anything about the plot to kill him or to blow up the body or the truck until later.

The defense attorney made much of this, and tried to get the jury to believe that Gomez was lying, that his whole story was a concoction, especially when Gomez claimed he was willing to knock out somebody but not kill him and that he didn't know that the plan was to blow up the jeep-type vehicle. Gomez stoutly maintained his story, however, and later, when it was corroborated by Casey, it seemed more convincing.

Gomez testified that he actually did hold Field about the arms, locking him from behind with his arms. Then, without Gomez having a chance to protest, Winters produced a large hunting knife and thrust it into Field's stomach. He said he pushed it back and forth, in and out of his stomach and chest until Field fell limply to the floor. He said that Field hardly struggled at all, because he seemed surprised at the initial blow with the knife, and didn't put up more than a few seconds opposition to the death grip which Gomez had on him from behind. After Field fell to the floor, Tom Winters had Gomez help him roll the body up in the rug that was there. They then called Casey and told him to hurry over, as he had been late.

Casey arrived to see, he said, the rug rolled up, and was told to help carry it out to the jeep. He had known that he was being hired, he said, to blow up a jeep, but never realized it was connected with blowing up a dead body too. He said he wanted to back out of the deal when he found out, but Tom Winters had threatened him too. He said that Winters told him they would in fact blow up the jeep anyway with the body in it and with Casey in it as well, if he refused to cooperate. He said he was so afraid of Winters that he agreed. He said he thought Gomez was cooperating too, but wasn't sure if Gomez was also afraid or part of Tom's inner circle.

Tom had Gomez drive the jeep, along with the body wrapped in the rug, to the range. He followed with Casey in the mechanic's pickup truck. Gomez said that he felt he had to do everything that Tom told him to do, as he was right behind him. Besides, he wasn't sure if Casey wasn't in on it all the time. Then, "there would be two against one, and what could I do?"

When they finally arrived at the spot that Tom had previously planned to use, he had Casey place a very large explosive charge directly under the seat where they had put Field's body. It was their thinking that if the explosive charge was big enough, it would totally destroy the body and the vehicle and make it appear as though Field had driven over an unexploded bomb driving in the night with his supply of illegal drugs. Field was suspected by the authorities anyway.

This would not be unusual, and they could get away with the whole crime.

Casey did in fact arrange the bomb on a time fuse. They set the fuse, drove off to what they thought was a safe distance, and saw the vehicle explode and burn. They were certain that no traces could possibly be left, and they returned to the condominium in Casey's pickup truck. Tom gave each of his co-conspirators six thousand dollars, keeping six for himself from the money they had paid Field. He kept the Cocaine for himself, telling them that he would give them any profits which might accrue from it at a later date. Both said that they never received any further payment and that at a later time, when they asked about the money, they. were told they were "lucky to be alive." Both said they were so much in fear of Tom Winters that they never raised the subject again.

It was not until more than six months later that Casey was apprehended by the FBI in connection with a careful evaluation of the explosion site. It became clear that there were no bomb fragments or shrapnel fragments. There were no other indications of a casing, nor any other material which would have been present had there been an unexploded bomb and the vehicle had run over it. In addition, the type of explosion and the force with which it had detonated indicated to the investigators that this was not the result of happenstance or an accidental wheel going over a detonating fuse of an unexploded bomb. It certainly was the result of a planned explosive device.

They had previously been investigating other terrorist type bombings. In fact, they had a list of detonation experts whom they suspected. Casey was on the list, and he was nearby geographically. They arrested him on suspicion of the explosion, and also told him that they could very well charge him with other unexplained explosions and extortion cases which they were currently investigating. He began to panic. He told them that it wasn't his idea and he had nothing to do with the killing at all. They told Jack that without any names or other evidence, they simply could not believe him, and were prepared to charge him with the whole crime. Under this pressure, he made a deal with the sheriff's investigators. In exchange for agreeing to turn state's evidence, he accepted a plea to a lesser charge. Ultimately, he gave them both Tom Winters' name and that of Aurelio Gomez.

When the investigators arrested each, they interrogated them both separately. Ultimately, Gomez too agreed to turn state's evidence in exchange for a reduced charge. In his case, the charge was reduced from first degree murder to second, since Gomez indicated that he did not know that the murder was premeditated or planned, but that it was simply to be an assault and robbery.

It had been almost a year by the time the case was completed and Tom was arrested. He did seem to have extricated himself somewhat from his financial problems by the time of his arrest, but whatever funds he had accumulated were quickly used up in his legal defense.

Ultimately, the case went to trial, and the jury chose to believe the two state's witnesses, Gomez and Casey, and, not Thomas Winters.

Tom Winters was eventually convicted of first-degree murder and sentenced to twenty-five years to life in the state penitentiary. Probably he is now preparing several appeals and also acting as a model prisoner. He is certainly bright enough to understand that this is the best way to shorten his stay in jail. It is quite likely that he will be released eventually on parole after the minimum statutory time has expired. Both Aurelio Gomez and Jack Casey are aware that this day will indeed come and too soon for them. They are probably even now making plans for this day, which is likely to be almost ten years away.

According to the jury's verdict, Tom Winters killed Eugene Field and blew up his body in order to cover up the crime. They felt the motive was greed and the acquisition not only of the cash which he had, but the goods which he had delivered in an attempt to shore up a shaky and failing business.

Curiously enough, greed is probably the rarest of motives for a killing. Most people kill friends or relatives or even strangers in fits of emotional stress or episodes of psychological agitation. Greed is the least likely motive for killing.

Lust, jealousy, fear and confusion are usually the cause. But, in this case, the pursuit of happiness became the pursuit of money and …

A NEW WORD FOR MURDER

CHAPTER 5

Hog Slaughter

Sexual perversion that leads to murder may be bizarre but is understandable. A distorted brain, whether it is through amphetamines and the burn-out of drug use can be fathomed. Somebody who is intoxicated and susceptible to irritability can kill. Even greed can lead to bad judgement and the taking of life. What about fear? Can you be so afraid in a situation that you will kill? Can a person be driven by terror to the ultimate act of destruction of another human being? Can we trace that blood red line into the heart of a small, timid and frightened woman? You will know the answer before you read the rest of this chapter. Could it happen to you, or someone you know, or even someone you love? Maybe so, and maybe not.

Raymond Hozzer was a big man. That is, he was big physically. He was about six feet tall and weighed two hundred and thirty-nine pounds "soaking wet," as he put it. He tended to be overweight, and he did not help it much by his eating and drinking, especially beer. His friends, in deference to his eating habits and to his general appearance, had named him Hog when he was still in the Army back in Korea in the nineteen fifties. At first, he objected to the nickname. But, after a while, it became a part of him, just as his bad back was something that he decided was something he had to live with and make the most of.

Hog actually did make the most of his nickname. After getting separated from the service in nineteen fifty-three, he worked for about four years as a truck driver and general handyman, finally injuring himself unloading a truck while working for the Acme Trucking Company in Little Rock, Arkansas, where he came from. After that he was really never able to work much more. He wound up on Social Security Disability and collected a check from then on.

At first, he saw the disability as something that was shameful. But, in the long run, it had its compensations. It allowed Hog not to have to punch a clock or keep schedules. Those were things he never enjoyed anyway. His disability gave him a lot more time to do the things he really liked to do. Among them was drinking beer. He sometimes could drink a six-pack in fifteen minutes. On one occasion, he remembered very clearly drinking two six-packs during the first quarter of a Redskin-Dallas Cowboy game. He had always been a Redskin fan as far back as he could remember.

At the beginning it was because the Washington Redskins, when he was a kid, were the only team in the National Football League that represented a town that was even close to being southern. Hog identified himself with the south since Arkansas was one of the original states of the Confederacy, he felt this was appropriate. He liked it even better in recent years when the Redskins started to win a lot and he could feel more comfortable.

Later on, when the Redskins went to the Superbowl two years running and had an offensive line called "The Hogs," he was "in Hog Heaven," as he put it. He walked around wearing a Redskin T-shirt and got decals to put on his pickup which said "Washington Redskins" and "Hog" and "Go Hogs." He even painted in red on the door of the cab of his pickup "Hog Heaven." The Redskins were his team, and he loved them. He went into mourning on the day that the Los Angeles Raiders beat them in the Superbowl, but he kind of suspected that that might happen. Afterall, the Raiders were a team owned by a Jew, and the coach was a "greaser." What could you expect from people like that? They didn't play fair.

They cheated. After a couple of extra six-packs of beer, he decided that his Skins would get them the next year. Besides, there probably were some more important things in life, although he couldn't think of them right at that time.

Hog was married. He had a wife, Billie Jo, and she was the mother of his two kids. He didn't think she was good for very much, except that she cooked "fairly decent." She came from back in Arkansas too, so she knew how to cook a little bit. Aside from that, she was always sniveling and crying and trying to spoil the kids. He made sure that the kids were not spoiled. He could keep them in line. But Billie Jo kept trying to get in the way and spoil them.

Recently, he had let their fourteen-year-old, Joanne, go to Sacramento to stay with Billie Jo's sister. She was going to go to school there because he couldn't put up with her sass and talking back to him and giving him a hard time. That is what he told the neighbors and the people he knew. Actually, Billie Joe had finally got up enough nerve to tell him that the kid would have to go there because Billie Jo was afraid he was getting a little too loose with his hands around his daughter's private parts. She thought that it was a sin, and it was going to hurt the child too. If he didn't do something like send her away, she was probably going to have to tell on him.

Hog and Billie Jo had a lot of trouble with sex anyway. She never really liked it, he thought, and he couldn't understand why she didn't turn him on. She didn't ever turn him on, except maybe when they first met right before he went into the Army. Everything after that was downhill, and it got to be that lately there wasn't hardly anything there at all.

Hog would go out sometimes and do what he liked to do most in the world.

That is, he would drive out to the desert and go out shooting. He would shoot rabbits and birds and small game, and he had a good time out there. He always enjoyed his guns, and he had a lot of them. He had a couple of rifles, and he had two really nice shotguns and even some pistols. He spent a lot of time with them. He would polish them and shine them up and check them out. He could take them apart and put them together just like they taught him in the Army, and he did it all the time.

He kept his weapons clean and neat. They were probably the only things he did keep clean and neat. Anyway, when he would go out in the desert, he would sometimes bring back some rabbits and some birds. He was putting food on the table. He would come back, and would have a lot of beer under his belly already, and he would want some sex. It sure was Billie Jo's fault that she didn't get him excited, though. He tried to have sex with her, get it on, and he couldn't perform. He would get a hard on for a few minutes, and it would just fall flat like an old hose without any water in it. He knew it was her fault, and he would really get mad at her. He would tell her she was no good, and she was flat chested, and she was ugly, and she had greasy skin, and he couldn't stand her. She would finally talk back to him enough, and he would smack her around a little bit.

There were only two times that Billie Jo had to go to the hospital. First was the time he broke her jaw when he hit her with the back of his hand, and maybe hit her a little too hard. Then there was that other time, that bad time, when she fell back and hit her head, and there was blood all over everyplace. She didn't move for a while, so he had to call the hospital and tell them that she slipped and tripped. That was when that nosey doctor got in the way and "called the sheriff" on him. They tried to file charges, but Billie Jo was smart enough to know that she wasn't going to testify against him. Afterall, a wife couldn't do that, could she?

It's against the Constitution of the United States for a wife to testify against her husband. He knew that, and he reminded her of it too, even though that wise- assed district attorney kid came around and tried to tell her that she could testify and she ought to testify against him. He told her how it was, and she kept her mouth shut.

The one time that he did get into trouble, he really could not blame Billie Jo, but it probably was her fault. That was the time that their kid, Ron, had to go to juvenile hall for stealing something. When he came back, he told Ron how stupid he was and how bad it was to get caught and how embarrassed Hog was. He showed him pretty good with his belt what the trouble was there. It was after that that the kid went to school and the teacher turned Hog in. Then he had to go to court, and he wound up doing thirty days in jail. Someday he would fix that teacher too. He used to tell Billie Jo about that, how he would get the teacher someday. He didn't care what would happen to him, he would just show the teacher that he couldn't go around and turn somebody like Hog in.

They lived in a mobile home park about forty miles out of town. Not everyone who lives in Palm Springs lives at one of the country clubs. There are a number of very famous and posh country clubs, including the Thunderbird Country Club, the Eldorado Country Club, the Tamarisk Country Club. There are also the Vintage, Morningside, The Springs, The Canyon, and literally scores of others. These are places where wealthy people spend their time and look forward to their retirement.

Since most people don't fall into that category even though they would like to, our multifaceted society provides compensation. You can still live in the "Golf Capitol of the World." You don't have to be a millionaire. You don't have to live at the golf course. There are a number of other available choices. The middle-class people live in middle-class homes similar to those you are familiar with all over the country, except they usually have swimming pools. It is not as expensive to build and install inground pools in the sandy soil of the desert. The linings never freeze or crack. Besides, you need one when you live in a place where the summertime temperature is one hundred degrees from June through September, and can go up to one hundred twenty-five degrees daily in the sun during the summer months.

The lower middle-class and people of even less opulent means live on the outskirts of the various towns between Palm Springs, Rancho Mirage, Palm Desert and Indio. They sometimes lived in mobile home parks near the major population centers. Sometimes they have to live even further away in places like Desert Hot Springs, Yucca Valley, Blythe and Thermal.

They all enjoy the climate of the desert, and those of course who live further out have some of the advantages of rural living and many of the disadvantages too. Hog and Billie Jo lived about as far out as you could live and still be in the desert. They were so far out that one of their more sophisticated neighbors pointed out that he expected to see the fort from "Beau Geste" appear any moment over the next hill. They were truly out in the desert.

Hog had some other troubles too. He got arrested a few times because some wise-assed cop or some pimply-faced deputy sheriff would come along when he was driving his pickup truck out on the back roads where he couldn't bother anybody and where nobody would get hurt, and just because he had had a few drinks and was drinking down some beer, they gave him those DUI's. He had three of them. The third time he had to go to jail for a while. That was okay except that he could not get any beer there. Then, there was the time that they said he had done "vehicular manslaughter." Some jerk had been driving on the wrong side of the road and crashed into Hog. He had got himself killed. Just because Hog had a record of those DUI's, they thought he was drunk when it happened. He beat that one, though.

Once, some guy in a bar room turned him in. The cops came along and told him he was guilty of public drunkenness, whatever that meant, because everybody else in the bar was drunk too. They're all a bunch of troublemakers, he knew that.

Altogether, Hog figured he wasn't such a bad guy, and he was misunderstood, and the whole society probably was against him because he was disabled and he couldn't work. Some people would put him down for that. But he figured his life wasn't bad. As long as he got that check every month and he had his pickup in pretty good shape, and he could see the Redskins for as many times as those New York Jews would let them be on Channel Two, he would be fine.

They did not always keep the Redskins on. They were showing some candy-assed teams like the New York Giants or those phony guys with the Dallas Cowboys, "America's team." They were not any more America's team than those sissy New York Jets with their Broadway Joe in his green suit. But he got to watch the Redskins enough, and the rest of the time he could watch the replays. He watched a lot of TV when he wasn't out hunting, and his life wasn't so bad.

Nobody ever told Billie Jo that she was a battered wife. The time that the district attorney and the deputy sheriff tried to get her to file charges against Hog, she didn't think it was the right thing to do even though she was in the hospital that time for two weeks. She thought maybe he didn't really mean it. But she was scared of him.

She later on said that she was probably scared all of the time. "It's kind of a funny feeling to be scared all the time. Maybe you can't understand it, but that's how I felt for the past ten to fifteen years. I used to be scared once in a while of Hog when he would drink and he'd get kind of mean and start talking crazy talk, and he'd sort of wander around. But I didn't think he was really a bad guy. It was right after Joanne was born that he started to get meaner, and nastier. When Ron was born, that's our little boy, well, after that there was no stopping Hog. He just got worse and worse. He couldn't have sex anymore. I'm not sure if he couldn't have sex because he drank so much and couldn't get it up anymore, or maybe he just wore himself out, I don't know. But he got meaner and meaner."

"It was after that that I was scared all the time. You know, ever since Hog died, I haven't been afraid anymore. Now it's even hard for me to remember how it was to be scared all the time, I mean daytime and night-time I'd wake up and be scared. I was just always scared. My body shook, and my belly was scared, and my hands were scared, and my head was most scared of all. I was scared that he'd get mean and he'd yell and he'd hit and he'd push. He'd smell always of the beer. His skin smelled like beer, his sweat smelled like beer. Everything. around him smelled like beer. I got so I hated beer and the smell of beer and even, God forgive me, the smell of my own husband. I hated the smell, and I think I got to hate him."

Billie Jo was only forty-two years old, but she really looked washed out.

When the doctor first examined her in the county jail, she looked like she was about fifty-five or sixty. There was a note in the doctor's original examination that said, "She looks ten to fifteen years older than her stated age," and she still did a few weeks later.

Her hair was kind of sparse and hanging down kind of straight. There was a lot of gray coloring, and it seemed to be full of split ends and almost a little on the messy side. Her skin was very pale, and this is unusual for someone who lived in California, out in the desert, all the time. Her skin was sort of a milky, creamy white, and there were blotches on it and a lot of wrinkles. She looked like she had lived a whole lifetime in her forty-two years.

When she talked about being scared all the time, one could look at her and see the worry lines and the wrinkles around her eyes and the creases around her mouth that looked like she was frowning most of the time. She was rather fidgety and more than a little jumpy. She sat in a chair being interviewed like a little bird that had been placed on a perch and wasn't really sure if it was safe or not. Her whole body seemed to quiver, even though she said she wasn't afraid anymore.

The doctor who examined her wondered what she looked like when she was afraid, and really could not imagine. She looked like someone who had been washed out of life. She appeared to be like a rag doll that had been thrown into a washing machine three or four times and wrung out of all color and texture.

There was no bounce left in her skin and no color in her hair. Even her eyes had a lusterless kind of flatness to them.

She was a sad case. She was a murderess. She had already confessed to shooting her husband. The real question was how and why and what to do next.

The only time that Billie Jo showed any life or any energy or any interest in anything was when she talked about her kids. Eleven-year-old Ron was the boy who was with her at the time of the shooting. He was now in a foster home in the Palm Springs area, and seemed to be handling things pretty well for an eleven- year-old who had just lost his father. Ron was in and out of school a lot because his father would tell him that he had to go with him to help him with his hunting. He didn't do well in school, but seemed to want to try, and was back in class.

Fortunately, the kids in school did not connect him with the story of the shooting, which happened down further in the Valley, so he didn't get teased about that. He was glad of it, and his mother was even more so.

Ron had been kicked around quite a bit by Hog. He didn't show any physical marks to look at him. But he looked like a frightened person. He had the kind of reactions that you see in people who are afraid all of the time. When you would reach out to shake his hand, he would cower and jump back. He would move his arms up in a protective way, as though he expected you to hit him. He was always looking about him, with his eyes darting left and right and his head moving around, as though he anticipated that someone might come up behind him and suddenly do something from the back to hurt him.

He was pretty skinny too. He didn't really have any meat on his bones. It looked like he didn't eat very much. If you offered him a candy bar, he would look around to see if anybody was going to take it from him, and then he would gobble it up very quickly. It was as though he thought he better do that before he didn't have it anymore.

We never got to see fourteen-year-old Joanne. Maybe that was just as well.

Billie Jo said she was doing real well there with her Aunt Mae. Mae lived in Sacramento with her husband who worked for the State and who was glad to take her. Mae didn't have any kids of her own, and "it was a blessing" for Mae to be there and to take Joanne with her and to let Joanne go to school and grow up "like a normal kid." Billie Jo was glad of this. She knew that Mae had explained to her what happened, that it was really an accident. He was always out hunting anyway, and that is what they told Joanne. They told her that there wasn't going to be a chance for her to go to the funeral because it was too far and too expensive. She seemed to understand that, and it didn't seem to bother her much.

Billie Jo said that she was pretty sure that Hog had touched Joanne and maybe fooled around with her a little bit. She never saw him do it, but once she saw Joanne crying. She knew what Hog was like. That was the one time she really stood up to him and got her back up and acted strong. At least, it was the first of the two times that she did that, and made him agree to have Joanne go and stay with Mae. She remembered arguing with Hog about this, and finally Hog gave in, saying, "Sure, send her up there to your flat-chested sister and her queer husband. They deserve that wimpy little girl of yours. She's like you, not me.

I don't need her around here. Get rid of her, get her out of here as soon as you can. All she does is take up time and space. We don't need her around here." That was Hog's farewell to his daughter.

Hog's farewell to life was somewhat more dramatic and, to him at least, more traumatic. Billie Jo told the story for the third or fourth time without a great deal of emotion.

"Hog was out there drinking again. He went out to the desert a lot. He took Ron with him, and he had one of those no-account friends of his. They went out to the desert a lot and drank beer and shot some little animals that nobody could eat anyway, and then they'd come back a day or two days later all liquored up to the gills and stinking, and he used to stink. I told you that already."

"Anyway, he came back that day, and he didn't even have any game. He didn't have a rabbit or a bird. He said that the weather was bad. He said the animals weren't around. He said that the shotgun shells were no good and a couple of them misfired. He had a lot of excuses. He always did for everything that went wrong. He told me he wanted me to cook up something for him to eat. I started to fix up some pork chops that I had in the ice box for him. I was going to make supper for him and for me and Ron and for Maybelle Anne. Maybelle Anne was the girl that was staying with us."

"I guess I didn't tell you about her, but she had a lot to do with it all. She was a twenty-one-year-old girl we had found out on the highway one day. People say she was touched or maybe crazy, but I think maybe she was just a little slow. Whatever the reason, she was on Social Security Disability too, and she got a check once a month. When she told us she didn't have any place to stay and could she share our mobile home with us as a place to stay, Hog was real glad. He said he'd be happy to take her in. He'd take care of her check and make sure she had a place to stay, and he'd always make sure she had a roof over her head and plenty to eat, and stuff like that. I think he was looking at the check more than he was at Maybelle Anne."

"But then later on, he started looking at her too, and that's what started all the trouble. Maybelle Anne wasn't bad looking. She still isn't bad looking. She's slow, like I told you. And she has kind of a hard time understanding things. But she knew about her body, and when Hog had trouble with me about sex (you know, he always did, at least, he did for the last fourteen or fifteen years), he started wondering if other women wouldn't be better for him'. I think he tried it a few times. He told me he did anyway when he was drunk. He said he was always good with other women. I don't know if it was true or not, or if he was lying. He lied a lot too. But then, I think he began to get ideas about Maybelle Anne. She was young, and she was full of piss and vinegar, and she laughed a lot and seemed to be a happy kid. I guess Hog thought she was going to save him. I don't know what she was going to save him for, but he thought she was going to save him, and he started to make up to her"

"But she wasn't that stupid. She wasn't that slow. She saw that he was a drunk, and she saw what he did to me. And she saw how he treated Ron. She saw how people didn't like him much, so she tried to stay away."

"The day that he came back and I was cooking up the pork chops, I served them on the table. I didn't really have any appetite myself. I didn't feel like eating nothing. So I told him I'd go out for a minute or two and see if the laundry on the line was dry. It was kind of a cloudy day. It was taking a long time for the clothes to dry on the line. I couldn't stand the smell of the beer oozing out of his skin and the sweat. Even the port chop frying was making me sick too. I went outside.

Little Ron came with me, because he wasn't hungry either. Hog and Maybelle Anne were sitting there eating the pork chops, the gravy and the potatoes. Hog was eating like he had never ate nothin' before. He must have had four or five pork chops. Maybelle Anne couldn't keep up with him, and she was eatin" pretty good too. Then, I went out to the line. The clothes were really still damp and there was no saving them right now, I'd have to go back later. I went right back inside, because I thought maybe I'd left the fire on the stove, and I was afraid there'd be a big grease fire. Hog would notice nothin' until it was too late. When I came in, I saw him. He was grabbin' at her, and he was puttin' his hand between her legs, and she was lookin' real scared and breathin' real hard. As soon as I opened the door, he pulled his hand away, and she got up and ran out the door, and sort of whimpered and cried. I told him. 'You have no call to do that, Hog.

You're goin' to scare that little child and you're goin' to lose your meal ticket too. She's goin' to get out of here as soon as she can, you dope.' I shouldn't have said that last, because that's when he whacked me again with the back of his hand. He had a ring on his finger too, and it cut me. You can see the mark here on my chin. I backed out, and he started mumblin' and grumblin'. He was gettin' real mean, and I knew he was goin' to do some real bad harm."

"Little Ron was outside, and I don't know where Maybelle Anne went, but I was real scared. Hog was rumblin' around. He was pushin' plates around and kickin' around the chair and screamin' that he was goin' to get me. He'd done that once or twice before, you know. He put me in a hospital once. He broke my jaw. I went back towards the pickup truck and sort a backed into the door. That's when I noticed the rifle. It was pokin' out the window. I figured it was there for a reason. I pulled it through the window and held it in my hand. I used guns before. I couldn't live all these years with that man without knowin' guns and how to use 'em. I felt better with it in my hands. I figured if he comes out here after me, I'm just goin' to point it at him and tell him to get away. So, I picked it up and had it in my hand, and I felt a little better."

"I felt better than I had in a long time. I thought to myself, all I need to do is squeeze this little trigger off in the right spot, and then old Hog he won't hurt me and he won't hurt Ron and he won't hurt Maybelle. and he'll never go near my little Joanne again either. While he was in there he was screamin' and rumblin' around. I heard him smash a bottle of somethin', and I figured he was lookin' for some more to drink. I figured pretty soon he's goin' to come out to the truck to look for some beer that he left in the cooler out here, 'cause there wasn't none left in the kitchen. Then he'd see me with the gun and he'd get real mad, and he'd probably try to take it away from me, and I wouldn't have the nerve to shoot it. I decided to just keep it with me, and I went around to the back of the mobile home. I still had the gun in my hands. I looked through the window, and there he was. He was mumblin' and grumblin', and I think he was maybe playin' with himself, I don't know. I just saw red, and I walked inside. He heard me, and he said, 'I'm going to kill you.' He was lookin' the other way. He didn't see me with the gun yet, and I knew he would. I just knew he would kill me, so I shot him. I shot him dead. It was self-defense. I had to do it, 'cause I knew he was goin' to kill me. None of these people here want to believe it, but that's exactly the God's honest truth, that's what happened. I shot him 'cause I knew he was goin' to kill me."

"I know I've never been much of a religious person, but I know God knows it's true. I don't know if God will forgive me, and I hope everybody else will understand, but I just had to do it for me and for Joanne and for little Ron and even for Maybelle Anne, and maybe even for all those little rabbits and birds and other stuff he used to shoot right out in the desert."

Billie Jo had given this confession before. She had told the deputies when they had come that she shot her husband because he was going to attack her. When they pointed out that it looked as though the shot had been in the back and had gone right through his back and through his heart and killed him instantly, she still insisted it was self-defense. She said unless you knew Hog you couldn't know how mean he was and how he tried to do everything he ever said. And that when he said he was going to kill her, he really meant it, that if she waited until he turned around and saw her with the gun, it would be too late for her. So, she shot him dead through the heart. She was a good shot.

Later, the sheriff's investigators got testimony from Maybelle Anne, who was a little slow. But she corroborated the testimony of Billie Jo, and said that most everything Billie Jo had said was about right. He had tried to put his hand there, and he did push her a little bit, and she got awful scared and ran away. She didn't know anything, except she heard a shot. He was always a mean fellow, but Billie Jo was real nice, and she knows that Billie Jo was only doing what was right.

They talked to Ron too. But Ron was outside when everything happened, so there really were no other witnesses. The neighbors and what friends Billie Jo had agreed that Hog was a pretty awful guy. They didn't really have to check that much, because all the police records corroborated his DUI's, his public drunkenness arrest, and his arrests for wife beating twice. There was also the business of the vehicular manslaughter, as well as the child abuse which was on record too from the school teacher's complaint.

So, most of the story seemed to be pretty logical. The only problem, of course, that faced the investigators and later the district attorney and the public defender was whether or not Billie Jo had acted in self-defense. It seems hard to take that position when a man is shot in the back from twenty feet away and killed with a single shot. He, of course, was in fact unarmed at the time. While it was true that blood samples taken right after the death indicated that he had a great deal of alcohol in his blood and extrapolation of the blood levels taken post-mortem indicated that he was legally drunk by far when he was killed, probably that is no reason to shoot somebody, at least, not in the sovereign state of California.

Hog Hozzer, without question, was a wife beater and a child abuser and a drunk. He was a destroyer of the environment, and a generally all-around bad guy. The only thing he did that was not bad was root for the Redskins. But he never paid a dime to go to a Redskin game, and he didn't even drink the beer that paid for the commercials on the network when the games were shown. He didn't pay a dime in taxes for maybe twenty years. And, in fact, he was drawing from the public treasury for most of his life. While there is such a thing as justifiable homicide, the ingredients listed above are not included among them. There really was not a good case for self-defense. The public defender could not go for that, and there was not really a case of temporary insanity, because while Billie Jo was battered and worn out and washed out and slowed down, she wasn't crazy. She wasn't crazy when she was examined. She wasn't crazy when she shot Hog, and she wasn't really crazy while she lived with him. Her mistake was to have lived with him at all.

One of the biggest problems that counselors and psychologists and psychiatrists have when they deal with battered wives is to get them to see the hopelessness of their situations. For some reason, they think that some magical change is going to occur and that the batterer is going to reform.

Usually, these men are heavy drinkers, users of narcotics or speed or some other illegal substance. Usually, they have no wish to change. Sending them to jail does not seem to do very much, and most of the time, the wives don't complain or press charges if they do complain. Child abusers are a little more readily taken care of because the state has set up laws so that school teachers and doctors and other concerned people can report child abuse and protect the child. Therefore, sometimes those men get put away even though their wives usually don't want to complain even then.

In this case, the older child did get protected and, ultimately of course, the mother instituted the final protection on behalf of the younger boy by eliminating the perpetrator, however violently and finally.

Eventually, after much discussion among the various attorneys and the courts and different doctors and social workers and probation officers involved, a plea bargain was arranged. Plea bargains, even though politicians keep saying they are against them, are probably the only thing that keeps our criminal justice system afloat. If there were no plea bargains, the courts would be ten times more jammed than they are now. Most cases would never get to court for speedy trials, and the criminals would have to go free anyway, because if you don't get a speedy trial in ninety days, your constitutional rights are being abridged.

In any event, the plea bargain was struck. Billie Jo, who was really so passive and washed out that she didn't make much of a statement of any kind on her own behalf, agreed to go along with her attorney's recommendation that she plead guilty to voluntary manslaughter. This is a crime which is not the same as premeditated murder. While it admits that the person charged with the crime did in fact kill the other person, the implication is that it was done for emotional reasons and in a moment of mitigation due to rage or fear or confusion.

Therefore, it carries a far lesser sentence.

Probably in Billie Jo's case, she will only have to serve the minimum amount of time because she never has had any criminal record before. She is so quiet and passive that she certainly won't get into any trouble in jail, and she is the kind of person, because of her family and background, and the like, who will get parole at the earliest possible moment. So probably after about three years, or maybe two, she will be released and, hopefully, she will be able to reunite with her children.

The tragedy, of course, probably extends more deeply to the children. It is hard to say what damage may have already been done to Joanne. Being molested by her father and being a witness to physical abuse on the part of the same father towards her mother and brother, as well as to herself, has got to be traumatic.

Some significant degree of damage unquestionably has been done to eleven-year- old Ron as well for all of the same reasons.

Billie Jo will probably remain a passive, frightened and withdrawn person but, hopefully, won't make the same mistake again. It is likely she will be sure to avoid that mistake by never marrying again. The likelihood of this crime being repeated is extremely remote, and that was taken into account in the judge's sentencing and in the probation report.

As for Hog, he probably was the victim of a lot of things. They included his upbringing, his background, his genetics, his weakness for alcohol, his unfortunate injury when he was a young man, and a society which allowed all these things to happen without really making any effort to do anything except put him in jail when he got too drunk, or rap him on the wrist when he did something excessive like attack his wife or children. His sexual problems are not unusual in child and wife beaters. Many men with this difficulty see themselves as needing to prove their masculinity and needing to establish a "macho" image. This is probably because they don't really feel they are very masculine or very effective or very worthwhile. They then try to establish their effectiveness by physical violence. It is hard sometimes to be violent with other men who are liable to hit back or carry a grudge and remember that you hurt them. But it is not so hard with little kids or with a little wife or with a passive, meek and timid family altogether.

You can really be the king of the hill inside your mobile home. But even then, sometimes the worm turns. In this instance, finally Billie Jo was pushed to the wall and committed ...

A NEW WORD FOR MURDER

CHAPTER 6

Five dollars a Bullet

Things are never black and white in life, and especially in this catalog of killings. As we have indicated on several occasions, they are frequently blood red if no other color. There is no one motive for anything, and we have been discussing mainly the outstanding motives; greed, fear, sexual lust, and drug abuse are among them.

Sometimes there is a combination, and sometimes the combination leads to a fatal result. One of the factors in the developing mosaic of the picture of a murder is panic. All of us are familiar with that feeling. It's the terror and the confusion and the agitation that happens when you're under great pressure and don't know what to do. Maybe it's the primeval instinct in all of us. We either fight or run. If we fight, we can kill. We are not that far out of the jungle that it isn't within us all to do so. If there is a weapon at hand, it makes it quicker and a lot easier.

It should be clear by now that understanding why someone kills never excuses the act itself. The goal in trying to understand the motives and backgrounds of the killers is to prevent future killings, not to condone those of the past.

Many times, it appears as if the killer is happy with what he has done, and only sad because he got caught. A bizarre situation occurs when the killer is truly repentant, has completely gotten "away with murder" and then decides, because of a sense of guilt or internal pressure or maybe some other reasons, to turn himself in. The following is an account of an unsolved murder which was solved by the killer himself.

A number of people in the desert area were very upset a couple of years ago about the death of "Red Mike." "Red Mike" operated a service-station on Highway 111, which leads into Palm Springs from the coastal area. There was a lot of talk at the local cocktail parties and gatherings, which occur so frequently in the desert resort during the winter season, about "Red Mike" and how he was killed.

"Red Mike" was found one night dead, having been shot through the head and killed in a robbery of his gas station. The body was found lying in the lube bay on its back, with a big hole blasted in the back of his head by what appeared to be a .45 caliber pistol.

As usual, the sheriff's department said they were "working on the case," but no suspects were found. Apparently, there were not very many clues. The murder occurred one evening in mid-week during the end of the spring season.

The "season" in the Palm Springs area traditionally begins after New Year's and runs through to' the end of April or into May. Usually, the weather in the desert is perfect at that time of the year. Daytime temperatures run in the seventies and eighties during the winter months of January and February and then in the eighties and nineties in March and April and into May. It is only at the end of May and beginning of June when the real hot weather comes and, of course, in the summer time it can get to be one hundred fifteen up to one hundred twenty-five by mid-July. By then, most of the tourists and visitors have gone, and only the "desert rats" remain through the summer.

This was late in the spring, so many of the tourists were still visiting. In addition, many of the "snow birds," that is, people who come into the desert during the wintertime when their home states are in snow, were still around. They would fly back North pretty soon but they, too, were aware of the story.

"Red Mike" had become a local character. It was only when people read in the newspaper about his shooting that anybody really got to know his last name. "Is that the same guy that used to have the station down on 111 on the way to Cabazon?"

"Yeah, that's him, 'Red Mike.'"

Nobody exactly knew how he got the name of "Red Mike." The second part was obvious. His name, as it turned out, was Michael Foran. Possibly, at some time earlier in his life his hair was red. Although when most of us knew him, his hair was pretty sparse altogether, and what there was of it was a grayish brown, at best. There was a lot of red in him, though. His skin was very florid, and there were lots of red veins which appeared on his nose.

Some people used to think he sat in the back of his gas station and drank quite a bit of the time. However, nobody ever saw him drunk, or even smelled booze on his breath, that we know of. Mike was a rather popular fellow in town because he made a point of remembering the names of his regular customers. He was able to do this mostly from the credit cards which they gave him. He would always address you by your name. The restaurateurs in town know that this is a method by which one can ingratiate himself in the minds of customers. They do it all of the time. Gas station owners do not usually think that way. But it paid off for Mike, because he had a popular station that was always busy, even during the summer when things slowed down for most places in town.

He seemed never to go home. He worked awfully long hours. People would go in at 7:00 a.m., and he would be there to greet them, and they were there sometimes as late as midnight, and Mike was there too. People thought he worked seven days a week, and I guess that was true, because nobody had ever recalled a day when the station was not open. He was "always there."

He used to say that if you would ask him if he would be open tomorrow, or on Easter Sunday, or on Christmas, or some other holiday, he would.

We never did know if Mike had a family, and no mention was made of it in the paper. Most of us thought he probably lived somewhere nearby or maybe even slept in the back of the station. It never was clear. The place would be closed late at night, and travelers who came into town after midnight would know that it was closed down. There was always a light burning in the back, but some people thought that was just a light to discourage burglars from breaking in.

Mike was not a very big man. He was not especially muscular either. He was a wiry sort of fellow, but he seemed to have enough energy to wrestle and bounce around the tires that had to be fixed from time to time. He had enough energy to loosen a frozen bolt if he needed to. He was generally able to handle the physical problems that came up in running that kind of a service station. He was not a mechanic, but he didn't pretend to be. If you had really significant mechanical troubles, he would refer you to somebody in town. He would even call them if your car couldn't go any further, and get them to take care of it.

Sometimes, when that would happen, Mike would like to talk to people while they waited to be picked up. Actually, there was not much of a conversation going on. It was Mike doing most of the talking about the affairs of the day, how he had to handle drunks and keep them calm, and how difficult it was to "work with the public."

In recent years, he was always complaining about "them kids," that is, the young people who came in sometimes, as he observed., "high on grass," or sometimes "speeding on Cocaine." Mike felt this was a sign of the deterioration of our society, and maybe he was right. He would talk about how it was dangerous to have these people around and that others didn't understand how serious this problem was, that is, unless they worked in a business like his where he had to come in contact with so many people all day long. He talked about these kinds of things while he checked your oil or washed your windshield. Then, as he filled out the gasoline receipt and gave you your credit card back, he said, "Thanks for coming in, Dr. Kurland, be seeing you again soon. With that big car of yours, I know you can't stay away too long, ha, ha."

Mike had never really felt very good about the self-service idea in gas stations that has swept the country. You know, the stations where you go in and fill up your own tank and then give the credit card or the money to a cashier. He felt this was going to ruin his "profession," but also knew that he had no choice. The big oil companies really dictate the policies that their owners have to follow. If the owners of the stations don't go along, they find themselves looking for another supplier. That becomes very hard when you get to be Mike's age. Most of us felt

Mike was somewhere between sixty and death or, at least, we used to say that when we would talk about him at the cocktail parties.

Of course, at the last party that Mike was talked about, he had reached the other side of that spectrum and was dead, and we all knew it had to be somebody who came in for some self-service gasoline, and then decided to help themselves to Mike's profits. Mike had been forced to install an island for self-service in his station, and while he said it took the personal touch out of his business and really stopped his ability to talk to people, he had no choice, and that's the way it was.

We all figured that Mike probably didn't have a chance to talk much to the robber. But then we figured we would never find out, because more than two years went by before anything else was ever said about "Red Mike."

About two and a half years after the killing, the desk sergeant at the Palm Springs Police Department got a telephone call long distance from Hawaii. It was from a young man who identified himself as Aubrey O'Neill. Mr. O'Neill said he was calling from Hawaii to confess a crime. He said it was important for him to talk to somebody about it, and when the sergeant asked him what crime, he said he didn't know whom he killed, but it was a gas station owner in Palm Springs, and it happened a little over two years ago. The sergeant said, "Just a minute, I'll get one of the detectives," and he connected the caller with somebody in the Detective Bureau.

When he did finally talk to a detective in the Homicide Squad, the young man indicated that he was the one who had shot Mike and that he was now feeling repentant. He wanted to confess the crime, and would they like to come over and arrest him? The detective got a lot of calls like this on a lot of murders. There are a number of murders in the desert, as most of my readers will know by now.

There are also, as you know, a lot of confessions for each murder. It sounded like this was another of those "confessions" from somebody who might be a little confused or possibly drunk, or maybe crazy out in Hawaii. So, the detective told him if he really wanted to confess to the crime and deal with his guilt, he should come back to Palm Springs and turn himself in at the police station and tell the story there. The man said, "That sounds like a good idea. I'll be there in a couple of days." The detective made a note of it, and figured he would never hear from that particular crazy again. Three days later, a man dressed in somewhat faded blue jeans and a bright red, yellow and green Hawaiian tropical shirt with pictures of palm trees and bougainvillea plants on it arrived at the front desk. He identified himself as Aubrey O'Neill, and said that he had come in response to his telephone call a few days earlier about the murder of the gas station man.

After listening to his story, the Detective Bureau was once again contacted, and his statement was taken. Aubrey was indicted for murder in the first degree.

Eventually, a public defender was assigned to the case in order to protect Aubrey's rights, and it became important for the defense attorney to get a psychiatric opinion concerning Aubrey. It is very unusual for a man to commit a murder, get away completely scot-free, and then surrender several years later simply to salve his conscience. This appears to be what Aubrey decided to do, however.

When Aubrey was visited in the county jail by the psychiatrist, it was not the first time he had ever spoken to a member of that profession. He was twenty- four years old, and for most of the first twenty-four years of his life he had been seeing psychiatrists, psychologists, social workers, mental health workers, and all of the assorted members of that profession.

Aubrey came from a well-to-do family in the mid-west. He actually had been born and raised in Chicago, and the earliest parts of his childhood were marked by his being always regarded as "unusual." He used to be very hard to manage. He never would listen to his mother, nor to the different babysitters, nor to the help that she got in to help her at home. It was very hard for his father to control him too. Sometimes they had to hit him to even get his attention.

However, this didn't seem to be a very useful tack to take, because he would have become a battered child in no time if, for every infraction, he would get a spanking.

Eventually, the family, when Aubrey was about four years old, took him to see a child psychologist. The psychologist felt that possibly Aubrey was jealous of his younger sister who was two years his junior and that this might have caused some of the difficulty. The psychologist gave him some toys to play with. They set up some doll houses and tried to work out the family dynamics.

Aubrey's father didn't think much of this kind of treatment, but since the mother felt it was "for the good of the child," he went along with it. The psychologist, after about two years of work, felt that Aubrey wasn't making very much headway at all, and when he had destroyed a number of the toys in her playroom and had attacked her a few times, she felt that possibly he needed to see a psychiatrist, and that even some medication might be appropriate.

Aubrey's mother was not very positive about the notion of medication. She had been reading a lot of columns in the daily newspaper and women's magazines about how foods were adulterated and preservatives had caused a lot of brain damage to children. She thought this probably was the cause of Aubrey's problems.

She did allow the psychologist to send Aubrey to one of her consulting psychiatrists, who felt that Aubrey might be a hyperactive child, and suggested some medication. Aubrey's mother did not want to go along with this, and the father felt probably they had been to enough doctors anyway, and they would have to handle it in their own way.

They sent Aubrey off to a private school after that, but it was only the first of several institutions that Aubrey visited. He never was able to be kept in one place very long. When he was seven, he had to be expelled from a school in Racine, Wisconsin, which was established to take care of "special children." This was because Aubrey set fire to the chapel one Tuesday night, using an accumulation of newspapers and even some prayer books that he found there. The people running the school felt that this was more than they could handle, and Aubrey was really too "special" for them. The family went through a number of other places, including when Aubrey was eight and nine, several military schools.

Nothing seemed to be very helpful.

Finally, when he was eleven, his parents' marriage had deteriorated so much (possibly due to arguing over him) that they divorced. Aubrey was given to the custody of the mother. It is questionable whether she had worked very hard to get it, but that is what happened. She moved to California with Aubrey to get away from bad memories of the Midwest and possibly also hoping that in some way the sunshine and warmth of the golden state would help her children to grow more fully and "more normally." Aubrey's sister, whom the parents had romantically named Dierdre, did not seem to have the same kinds of troubles that Aubrey did, but she was angry at all the attention and time that the family lavished upon her older brother, who was "just a bad boy," as she put it.

Moving to California didn't seem to change things too much, but Mrs. O'Neill at least decided to put Aubrey in the public school system and try to keep one environment the same for him all the time. The public school had a considerable amount of difficulty with him, but by this time, he seemed to have calmed down a little bit and confined most of his mischief making to home and to after school.

It wasn't until he was fifteen that he got into serious trouble again. That was when he stole the neighbor's Rolls-Royce. The neighbor, of course, was enraged about this, and did not take it very kindly when the car was found on the other side of town all scratched up from being unable to negotiate a turn near a stone wall. Aubrey was sent to the juvenile authorities, and it was finally decided that he probably needed to go to an institution. Aubrey's mother, by this time, did not fight that very much, and she agreed that he was "incorrigible."

When Aubrey was at the Juvenile Hall, he was given some mandatory tests by psychologists there. They agreed that he had some significant problems and possibly some of the rough and tumble things that he had done as a child, including a number of falls and possible minor head injuries, might have some relationship to his subsequent behavior. They suggested that he might have some kind of organic brain syndrome of a minor nature, and asked for a neurological evaluation. Aubrey's mother was delighted that someone had an idea and an explanation but, unfortunately, the neurologist did not add anything to the picture. In fact, he said there was nothing major defined, and suggested more detailed neuro-psychological testing.

Aubrey's mother was willing certainly to look into this too, and arrangements were made to have Aubrey sent to an institution in Texas which had been established for the evaluation and treatment of problem children.

When he was there, he was seen by the entire staff. It was once again established that Aubrey probably had some mild signs of neuro-psychological damage, and maybe the multiple head injuries he had suffered in his youth might explain some of his behavior. In any event, he was placed on some stimulant medication which has the paradoxical effect in kids with this kind of disorder of calming them down. This, plus something to help him sleep at night, because the stimulants tend to keep people awake if they take enough of them to calm them down during the day, seemed to help.

Aubrey calmed down and went along with the program, and he seemed to be doing quite well through his entire sixteenth year. The mother was becoming very encouraged, but it was finally decided that Aubrey had to leave the school when he was seventeen, as he was "too old" to remain in that particular institution. They suggested that possibly he could simply go ahead with outpatient care.

Mrs. O'Neill agreed that Aubrey would return home and finish his last year of high school in California. Aubrey really never made it through high school, though, because shortly after coming home and, of course, not taking the medication which had been prescribed, he "took off" once again.

Aubrey began a series of stops which took him to Idaho, Montana and Nevada. He especially liked Nevada, and particularly liked Las Vegas. He said it was the kind of place where people didn't pay much attention to his own peculiar traits or personalities because "everybody was high there." He spent a good deal of time there, at least until he was arrested for "joy riding" in some cars which he had been parking for one of the hotels. He got a job, parking cars, which lasted for two weeks until somebody came in with a bright red Excalibur. Aubrey just thought the Excalibur was the neatest thing he had ever seen, and decided to take it out for a spin. That might have been okay, except that wasn't the most careful driver in Nevada. He ran it off the road on the highway outside of Vegas and couldn't get it started again. By that time, of course, the police had been informed, and Aubrey was arrested for grand larceny, auto.

Because he was still a juvenile and didn't have any major prior record, Aubrey was placed on probation and told to go to a mental health clinic in Las Vegas. He did do that until he was eighteen, and then feeling he was now free of the restrictions of the court, simply left Nevada and returned home.

Nobody appeared to pay a lot of attention to him at that point, and so from the ages of eighteen to twenty, he spent a lot of time in Southern California, moving from city to city and job to job. He never had any really skilled job, but was able to always go home and borrow some money from his mother. By this time, Mrs. O'Neill had written him off, and felt that if she could just give him a few dollars from time to time and keep him out of her hair, he might sooner or later "grow out of it and grow up."

When Aubrey finally made it to Palm Springs, he got a job at one of the local restaurants as a busboy. Later on, when he expressed his interest in cars and showed that he had a valid driver's license, he was given the opportunity to park some. He loved this job, and didn't get into any major trouble "joy riding," because "I had learned my lesson by that time." Unfortunately, however, he did start to use drugs and especially "speed." Aubrey remembered that when he had taken speed in the hospital under controlled conditions, it had made him feel pretty good, and he thought if he took some more, he would feel even better. He got a hold of some "crack," which is a homemade form of amphetamine, and liked it very much indeed. He started to take it on a regular basis, and noticed that when he took it, he could do his job even more quickly and more efficiently. His tips went up, and he had more money, so he felt it was a good investment.

Unfortunately, Aubrey had to buy more and more "crack" to keep feeling good, and he began to find that his funds were short. This necessitated thinking of other ways to get money. After some reflection, it occurred to him that there were so many rich people in town who didn't deserve to be so wealthy, that he would try to even things out. The latter day Robin Hood began a series of small- time robberies, stealing from houses near the restaurant, and mainly trying to find things that were quickly negotiable. If he found cash, of course, that was ideal. Sometimes jewelry and small radios and even a few T. V. sets were available.

He didn't steal regularly, and after a while, he began to realize that he couldn't keep stealing in the same neighborhood or he would get caught. He began to move further and further away from his base of operation. Finally, on one occasion, he found a .38 caliber revolver in one of the houses that he burglarized, and took this too. It was when somebody saw him with the revolver (which he decided not to pawn but to keep "for an emergency") that he was finally arrested. This time Aubrey did have to go to jail.

He spent about a year in prison, but got out as soon as the law would allow because he was such a model inmate. He never got into any trouble. He got along with everybody, and he was polite and pleasant, and did not appear to be a hardened criminal. He was released after about a year, and came back to Palm Springs to celebrate his early release. It was at this time that he ran into some of his old friends who used to work with him at the restaurant, and they decided "to have a party."

Aubrey was never one of your intellectual types. He didn't really spend a great deal of time thinking things through, and he tended to be somewhat impulsive about almost everything. He was not the kind of person who read a lot. He was never the kind of person who spent a great deal of time in conversation with others. He was impatient, impulsive, and very emotional. His friends felt that his emotional qualities were endearing and charming because he would get very excited about things.

He would become very enthusiastic about almost any project that they had proposed. This went for "joy rides" and fun and sometimes illegal activities. His emotionalism had many dimensions besides being enthusiastic and excitable. He would laugh a lot, and sometimes when somebody told him a joke that wasn't very funny, he would laugh for two or three minutes at a time, thinking it was the funniest thing he had ever heard. In a way, of course, this made him popular with people. This was especially true with those who liked to tell jokes, and many of his friends liked to have him around at parties because of that. He wasn't a bad looking fellow, being about six feet tall and rather slim. He had a nice complexion and sort of brownish-red hair, and a lot of the girls he hung out with said he had a "kind of a dreamy look." They thought he was sort of romantic and "like a poet." It is doubtful that Aubrey ever read any poetry and unlikely that he ever read a book, including Robin Hood. "But I did see it on T. V."

He did like to listen to poetry, and when some of his friends would talk about it, he would smile and listen and say, "Yeah, that's deep, really deep, I really dig that, man, I dig it." Altogether, Aubrey was the kind of guy you liked to have at parties. He would get angry sometimes and explode, but most of the guys at the parties could handle that, and he would calm down right away too. He could sometimes get very sad when people sang sad songs or told sad stories, or how unhappy their lives had been. He would feel awfully sorry for them, and cry for them too.

He would tell them sometimes about how his family broke up when he was a kid and how he thought maybe it was his fault, and he would cry a lot then as well.

So, when Aubrey got out of jail, everybody knew about it, because he had written to some friends, and they were waiting for him. They had a big party, and it lasted for about a day and a half. Most everybody got drunk at the party, especially Aubrey. In addition to booze, there was a lot of grass around. While that wasn't his favorite, it was something that would make him feel good and, after all, after a whole year of deprivation, it was a pretty good idea.

Later on, Aubrey couldn't remember much of anything about what happened during the party or right afterwards. He thinks that he was with a girl that time. He said he wouldn't be surprised if that were the case because he had "been like a monk for so long." But he isn't clear about that either. The only thing he does remember is that the day after the party, he was walking around town sometime in the morning when he was picked up by the cops. He knew he hadn't done anything, although he didn't remember very much very clearly, so he was surprised when they took him in. He thought maybe they had arrested him because he looked drunk. He knew he hadn't done anything and, sure enough, the next day they let him go. Apparently, they thought he had been involved in another burglary, but he wasn't very clear about any of these events.

After being in jail once more for twenty-four hours, he felt that he had really been mistreated. He went to see some of his friends as soon as he got out again. Fortunately, he found somebody at a bar who was willing to share a quart of vodka with him. They sat around drinking vodka for more than a couple of hours until it got dark. Then Aubrey figured that he had to start making some plans to get some work or to do something to get some money to live his life. They both thought maybe they would go over to one of the fancy restaurants in town and see if they were looking for people to park cars. His friend pointed out, however, that he doubted they would give him a job in his present condition, because he still seemed to be kind of woozy from his half of the bottle of booze. So, the friend decided not to go.

Aubrey went anyway, and when he got to the restaurant, he realized that his friend was probably right, because he had trouble walking steadily. He figured it was a good thing it was dark, or the cops would probably pick him up again and keep him in jail for another night. He decided to walk around to the back of the restaurant, and that is when he saw the Mercedes. It was a brand new, chocolate brown Mercedes sedan, with brown leather seats and the little Daimler-Benz decal stuck on the inside windshield that they have on the brand, new ones. It looked beautiful. The keys were still inside. Apparently, one of the guys who parks cars had left it behind the restaurant for a few minutes, figuring he would pick it up again soon and deliver it to the customer who was finishing his dinner.

Aubrey thought it was a waste to let some fat old rich guy drive around in a car like that when he didn't even have any wheels at all. He decided to borrow the car and take it for a ride. Aubrey had never stolen a car in order to resell it, although he had resold other things in his life that he had, stolen. Cars were a little out of his league. He pointed out that his main interest in taking the Mercedes was to drive it around for a while "to feel good." He had always felt good when he had taken cars before, and he thought this would be something he could do, take the car and drive it around for the evening. He would then leave it someplace where the owner would find it with the vehicle no worse for the wear. He got in and drove it away.

As he started to drive toward Highway 111, he thought it might be a good idea if he took the car to Los Angeles and seek his fortune there. He was about to leave town when he noticed there was hardly any gasoline in the car at all. What thoughtlessness on the part of the owner! He would probably have run out of gas himself if Aubrey hadn't taken it. He stopped at this Shell station he saw on the highway. It was a self-service type of station. He could get some gas there, fill up the tank and go into the city. He stopped and pulled up in front of one of the pumps, and realized he had only five dollars with him. He had four singles and a dollar's worth of change, and what with the price of unleaded gas these days, it wouldn't go very far. He gave the cash that he did have "to that little skinny bald guy in the station." He told him he'd take five dollars of gas.

The guy said, "Go ahead and help yourself." Aubrey kind of laughed, thinking that maybe he would have to help himself, sure enough. He put ten dollars of gas in the tank, figuring that would be enough to get him into Los Angeles, and worry about what to do after that. He got back into the car as soon as he had put the nozzle back on the pump, "but that little guy was fast. He ran up to me and pulled open the front door of the car and said, 'Where do you think you're going, sonny?' He told me to stop, and he said that I owed him five dollars more, that I had taken five dollars too much worth of gas. I told him I'd give it to him tomorrow morning, that I just didn't have any more money. He didn't seem to be satisfied with that. He told me to pull the car over into the lube bay right away, so I did."

After Aubrey had pulled the brand, new Mercedes into the lube bay, the little skinny guy took the keys out of the car so he couldn't go anywhere, and put them in his pocket. He told him he'd be back in a few minutes. Aubrey wasn't sure what he was going to do, but he had a thought that maybe this guy might wind up calling the cops on him. He figured that most people seeing somebody in a new Mercedes would give them credit for five dollars at least and let them go on their way, but not this guy.

He started to get a little scared, and he figured he would look around the car and see if the owner had left some money in there. He looked in the glove compartment and didn't find any money, just some old maps and a service booklet. He even looked under the seats on the floor, and only found thirty-five cents. That wasn't going to satisfy the old guy. He looked in the side pocket, and he found a .45 caliber Colt automatic. It was loaded. He thought that might be some kind of a sign. The gun was the answer to his problem. He could sell it to somebody for a lot of money. The old guy was in the little shack near the gas pump. He was locking up the cash box. "I just walked over behind him and didn't say nothing. I just pulled the trigger." Aubrey shot him through the back of the head. It actually blew "Red Mike's" head in half.

He swears that he didn't think about it beforehand, and he swears that he didn't plan it at all. He just pulled the trigger and shot the guy, and one shot was sure enough. When he shot him, he blew forward maybe two or three feet, and there was a big chunk of his skull gone. He knew he had killed him.

After he had done that, Aubrey realized he had really gotten into trouble this time. Nobody seemed to have heard the shot, but he knew he had to get the keys back from the guy's pocket, so he reached in the pocket of the dead body, and got the car keys. He also remembered the cash box. It was somewhere nearby, and he was going to need money for his getaway. He went inside the little room where the man had come from, and found the tin box with about one hundred dollars in it, and he took that too.

Aubrey got back in the car, and figured he better not try to leave town. It would be too easy to find him. He drove back into Palm Springs and threw the gun into a construction site where it looked like they were going to be pouring some concrete pretty soon. He put it underneath some dirt and left it there. He then tried to wipe off all the fingerprints and marks, and anything else he could think of that might indicate he was in the car. He left the chocolate brown Mercedes a few blocks from where he had taken it. He then walked over to where the rest of his friends had been staying and asked if he could stay with them for a couple of days until he could get himself straightened out. He had a hundred dollars in his pocket, and he knew that he could take care of himself for a little while anyway.

By the end of the week, when it was clear that nobody was really looking for him and when just the story in the paper about the shooting had appeared and nothing more was said, he thought it might be a good idea to leave town. But, by then, almost all of his money was gone, so he called his mother in Pasadena and asked her if she could give him enough money to go to Hawaii. As usual, his mother thought that was a pretty good idea and that that might do him some good. Since he had always been in so much trouble in California and on the mainland altogether, maybe Hawaii would help him. She sent him the money, and he flew to the Hawaiian Islands.

When he got there, he found a job in a hotel as a busboy, and he liked it very well. He didn't seem to have as much trouble in Hawaii as he had had in California, and besides it was easy to get marijuana there and it was good stuff. He felt calm most of the time. He also found God while he was in Hawaii, or at least that's how he felt.

Aubrey was living with this lady, who was a little bit older than he, maybe thirty-five or thirty-seven, he isn't sure. She was warm and loving and kind, and she was "into Bahai." She was a real believer in the Bahai faith, and converted Aubrey too. He started listening to her and talking to her friends. He became more and more convinced that there really was a God and that God was love and that he should become more religious. He became very emotionally attached to his lady friend and also to her faith. He finally told her of what he had done in California. She convinced him that the only thing to do was to make a clean break of the whole thing and to try to be forgiven by God, and to confess his crime and never do evil again. With this in mind, after two and a half years, he called the Palm Springs Police Department. Then later, with the money he had saved from his job, he flew back to California to confess the crime.

Later, the district attorney felt that possibly Aubrey had been less than honest in his story. No one could ever prove, of course, that he "found the gun in the pocket of the car." The district attorney, in his presentation of the case, tried to make it appear that Aubrey had had the gun with him all along. He believed that Aubrey had, from the beginning, planned to rob the gas station and shoot the owner if he resisted, or maybe if he didn't, so he would not be a witness. He insisted that it was a premeditated murder.

Since Aubrey had already committed the crime and confessed to it, there wasn't any need to have a jury trial. Besides that, since it was reasonably clear that Aubrey was not psychotic either at the time of the examination nor at the time of the commission of the crime, there was not really any need for a sanity hearing either. It was finally agreed that a judge would decide whether or not Aubrey had committed first or second-degree murder. First degree murder means that you kill somebody with premeditation and with the intent to do so before the crime is committed. Second degree murder means that you kill them but that that was an impulsive and an emotional act, rather than a planned-out, premeditated and vicious one.

In Aubrey's case, the judge agreed that Aubrey was not the type of person who ever planned anything out and that while he had committed a vicious and horrible crime, he probably didn't think it through in advance. He opined that Aubrey probably had never had the ability to form an intent for anything in his life, whether it be a murder, the "joy riding" of a car, or even getting drunk and falling on his head. As a consequence, he sentenced Aubrey to fifteen to twenty- five years in the state penitentiary for his second-degree murder.

It is likely that after the minimum time in jail, which would be eight or nine years, Aubrey will be eligible for parole. At that time, because he has always been a model prisoner, he probably will be released. Aubrey is the sort of person who seems to be very likable, and no doubt will get along with everyone in jail.   He will be liked by them all, the jailers, the prisoners or anyone else he comes into contact with. He is also the kind of person who can't tolerate any kind of drugs.

Whether they are alcohol, marijuana or stimulants or depressants, Aubrey reacts to them. He probably does have some minor kind of brain damage, as indicated in the studies which were done when he was an adolescent. But these are not an excuse for murder or for anything else, for that matter. It just helps us to understand him.

There are a number of people around like Aubrey, who are rather volatile in their emotions. That is, little things can make them go from happy to sad and from angry to compassionate within a few moments. The important thing to understand about them is that they are extremely sensitive and susceptible to any kind of outside influence, and even more so to booze or to drugs. Probably these chemicals played a major part in what happened to him. Probably if Aubrey could have been kept completely away from these substances, he never would have killed "Red Mike." Probably "Red Mike" would still be pumping gas and cleaning windshields and checking oil for his regulars in Palm Springs and for the tourists who came in the wintertime. Maybe if "Red Mike" hadn't been concerned about that extra five dollars of gas that this "wise kid" had pumped, he would still be around complaining about all the kids and troublemakers. But this time, instead of getting the dollars, "Red Mike" got a bullet, and Aubrey committed ...

A NEW WORD FOR MURDER

CHAPTER 7

Closet Killer

Killing is forever and murder is for keeps. The act of murder is for real and can never be condoned under any circumstances. Sometimes you can't help but feel sympathy for the murderer as well as the victim. Often it appears that the murderer is the victim himself or herself, in some cases. In this case, the cause of the killing probably started at the beginning of the killer's life and even before that, with his father and maybe his father before him. Even what appears to be the most cold-blooded and premeditated of crimes doesn't seem that way when you get all of the details. Some killers can really be insane and still carry out their deadly deeds throughout, and because of their madness. Even the madness itself can be triggered by things going on in their lives which seem to be beyond their control. An inability to understand the opposite sex, a yearning for love and a hunger for warmth which has never been fulfilled can lead to insane jealousy and rage and, who knows, even actual insanity. The words to the popular song, "You, You're Driving Me Crazy" can be all too true, except the tragic result can be that the one who is driven crazy can also kill.

Gary Lomak was a product of a blue-collar family from Northern New Jersey. He. never got many breaks, and he had to make the ones he did get for himself. He was born in Jersey City, New Jersey, an industrial town across the harbor from Manhattan. He was an only child, and later his mother felt that this was probably a good thing and "a blessing from God."

Gary's father worked in a can company in Jersey City. His dad didn't make a great deal of money, but always "made enough to put meat and potatoes on the table," or so Gary remembers him saying. His father was never a very happy man, and felt that the only joy and satisfaction he could get from life was in coming home and drinking some beer and going out on weekends and "hangin' out with the boys." His father liked to play football on the weekends with a local sandlot team. He prided himself on being "almost good enough to make the pros." George Lomak never had a chance to go to college, and in fact he never finished high school. George still thought that he was a pretty good football player, and maybe he was. Gary really never got to know him very well, so can't say even now. His parents divorced when Gary was nine.

Gary's mother came from a middle-class family in New Jersey, and they always felt that she married "down" when she found his father.

When they finally divorced, it was because she was certain that "George Lomak was fooling around with anything in skirts." She decided to leave Jersey City forever. It was her idea to get as far away as she could from the scene of her shame and her divorce and her failure in her marriage. She decided to move out to California. She had saved up a few dollars, and borrowed a little bit more from her own mother, and she and little Gary went off to the West to make a success.

It wasn't easy for Margaret Lomak to make a success. She had finished high school, but she had no skill and no special talent that she knew of. She did know how to work hard, and she knew if you stuck to things and tried, things would work out. Her first jobs were as a waitress in a variety of restaurants. She worked

her way up from some of the small chain-type restaurants, where the tips were small and the hours were long, to some of the fancier places in Beverly Hills. By that time, she thought she was in fact making it pretty well, and she started saving her money. It was her hope that after she got enough money together, she might be able to own her own place. She eventually became a part-time manager of one of the better restaurants in Beverly Hills.

As the years went on, eventually she had the opportunity to buy into "a nice place" in Palm Springs. Because it is a resort town,

Palm Springs has a large number of restaurants. There are Chinese, Japanese, Italian, French, Greek, Kosher, "Continental" and even some Scandinavian places. Besides the Mexican Taco Houses, "English Style Grills" and "Mid-Eastern Cuisine" eating places, there are a few in-between, middle-class "American Steak Houses." They cater to the Mid-American tourist group. These are the folks who begin to blame their heartburn and indigestion to "all that foreign food," instead of the wine, beer, Margaritas, ouzo, Saki, plum wine, vodka and bourbon they consume on their holidays. Instead, they go to "a real American place" to settle their stomachs. Mrs. Lomak was the hostess and part owner of the re-christened "Margaret's Place." Business was good, and the profit margin was adequate. God had finally looked with favor on Margaret Lomak in the second half of her life. Or so she thought.

It appeared that Gary was built more like his mother than his father. That is, he was not a really big man, and it didn't look like he was going to be capable of great physical labor throughout his life. He was strong and wiry, and he made the most of his physique. His mother kept saying to him that she hoped he had wound up with her brains too. She never did think much of the ones his father possessed. One of the problems that Margaret had throughout her life was that she never could stop pointing out to Gary how his father had botched up her life and his own as well. By extension, she also felt that George had botched up Gary's life, and she was going to do her best to straighten it out. Gary remembered, however, that she kept telling him "over and over again" what an inadequate person his father had turned out to be. She pointed out on a number of occasions that it was up to Gary not to make the same mistakes George had made. It was one of the things that Gary kept in his mind all of the time. That is, that he didn't want to ever have to turn out to be like his dad. His mother never let him forget that.

Gary tried hard in school because of these feelings, and he got fairly good grades. Even though he was only average in' intellectual capacity, he managed to get a high B average, and hoped to go to college on a scholarship. His mother, by that time, had just bought into the restaurant in Palm Springs, and at first didn't have a lot of spare cash to send Gary to school. She told him that if he couldn't get a scholarship to the University of California or to some private college, including tuition, she didn't think she could help him. She might be able to help out with room and board, but that was about all.

Gary tried the best he could, but it never really did work out. He wasn't able to get a complete scholarship, and had to finally settle for a junior college and a part-time job in the restaurant.

All through high school, Gary spent most of his time and energy proving that he wasn't too bad. It really turns out that Gary never did have a very positive attitude towards his father and, by extension, for most men. There never was any specific father figure in the house, because Margaret decided that she would never remarry again. She felt that one bad marriage was enough in anyone's life. She decided that she was going to stick to her career and get involved in the "really important things in life." She meant by that, hard work and success, and saving and living a clean life.

Margaret became a regular church-goer, and got more and more involved in her religion. She became extremely religious finally, and began to feel that she was in fact "born again." She knew that this was a glorious thing to happen to her. She hoped it would happen to Gary someday too. Margaret tried not to talk about his father anymore, hoping that she could put all this behind herself and Gary as well. Nevertheless, it was very hard for her not to mention, every once in a while, that Gary should try not to be a bum and a loafer and a failure, like his father.

Gary always was afraid he would turn out to be like him.

Gary felt that working hard in school was one way to do this. As a result, he didn't have enough time for athletics and sports, but since that was his father's thing anyway, it wasn't that important. He tried to keep in good shape, and made a pretty good physical appearance even though he wasn't a real athlete.

Gary had a normal interest in girls, and he dated from time to time. He didn't want to waste all his money on dates. But he did have some extra income that he got from working as a busboy in his mom's place, and he would go out with girls to movies and dances and school activities. He was always looking hard to find a girl who was "clean and wholesome." He felt there were too many girls in high school who were "into dope" and other unwholesome activities. He didn't think that sex itself was unwholesome. It was easy to be tempted in high school to get involved in sexual activity. But Gary knew it wasn't right, and he thought it would probably be better to wait for the right girl.

Gary "stuck to his guns," and he finally did meet someone in junior college whom he thought was clean and wholesome and right for him. Janet was eighteen years old, and was going to junior college so she could learn to be a legal secretary. She thought maybe she could do this or be a court stenographer, or something like that. She was very sincere, energetic and hard working. Gary thought she was bright and ambitious just like his mom, and had all the right qualities for a wife.

Margaret thought that possibly Janet was too young for Gary and that he, too, was too young to consider any permanent relationship. She advised that the two young people wait until they had finished school. Then, they could see if they still cared for each other before they made any permanent commitments.

The pressure of love and sex and being eighteen was too much for both of them. They finally decided that getting married would be the way to handle their problems. They didn't want to keep having sex in an "illicit" way, the way they had been lately. They agreed that if they were married, they could keep their jobs and still work and go to school and complete their careers. So, they got married with her family's blessings and his mother's somewhat reluctant agreement. They got married in church the way Margaret wanted, and she cried at the wedding.

Afterall, it was her only child, and she felt that maybe Gary would turn out okay in the long run. The girl seemed to be the right kind of level-headed person that men needed to keep them in line.

Both Gary and Janet had jobs by now in a local supermarket. This allowed them both to go to junior college and make some money and support themselves as well. One of their problems, though, was that their hours were not always the same. They were taking different classes in school, and they were interested in different directions. Gary wanted to learn how to be some kind of scientist, and was taking a lot of courses in engineering and physics, and that kind of thing. Janet was still interested in some kind of legal career. Their job hours were not the same either, and they sometimes didn't get to see each other until very late at night. This continued for a while until Janet got pregnant.

After a few months of pregnancy, Janet realized she couldn't continue in school and keep her job too. She finally had to drop out of school. Later, she had to stop working as well when she got too big to be able to work in the supermarket. They finally had a little boy, named Gary Jr. They both hoped they would have more time together and also time with the baby.

It didn't work out that way. Gary Sr. was feeling the pressure of having to support his wife and child without Janet's income. He had to try and work more and more hours. He took an extra job delivering the L. A. Times to subscribers in the Palm Springs area. That meant that he had to get up around three in the morning to go pick up the newspapers and then distribute them between the hours of four and six. By about seven a.m. he was pretty beat, but then he had to get ready to go to school. Then, after school, he had to go to his job at the supermarket. By the time he was through, he wound up getting only four or five hours sleep a night. On weekends it was just as bad, because the supermarket needed him to work those hours more than they did during the week. The Sunday papers were a big load as well. The L. A. Times on Sunday is probably five to six times bigger than the daily paper. By the time Sunday afternoon came around, Gary was too tired to even look at the pro football games on T.V.

All of this pressure began to lead to more and more friction. Janet was angry because Gary didn't have time to help her take care of the baby. The baby was kind of a crier and a whiner. He would stay up late at night crying and waking up Janet. Gary was either "dead to the world" or gone by three o'clock to do his newspaper job. They began to fight. When the baby was only six or seven months old, Gary began to get suspicious that maybe Janet was "fooling around" with one of the neighbors.

There was a man who lived in the next apartment who was separated from his wife. Gary always thought that the neighbor had eyes for Janet. Since Gary was away so many hours and so much of the time, both day and night, he could not control his suspicions. He began to ask Janet if the neighbor had been in once in a while and if he was spending time there. Maybe he was playing with the baby. Or maybe he was perhaps better looking than Gary, and so forth. At first, Janet denied everything. But finally, she said she had talked to the neighbor, and he probably was more interested in Gary Jr. than Gary Jr.'s own father was. This created even more dissension, and things started to go from bad to worse. They got some counseling from the pastor at Margaret's church, but that didn't seem to help very much. Finally, Janet took off one day with Gary Jr., and went back to live with her family.

Gary's mother told Gary that probably he was too young in the first place to get married. Besides that, he was only twenty years old now, and he had his whole life before him. She said everybody was entitled to a mistake, and hadn't she done that too? She tried to reassure him. Gary really felt down, and figured he had really botched things up the way his father had.

Gary began to think of ways out of all this overwhelming pressure, and it dawned on him that there was one pretty good solution. He always had hoped to get an education, but felt he couldn't piece it together with all of his responsibilities. Since he never did get a scholarship to college, there must be some other answer. He started seeing the television ads telling young men to join the army and the navy and get an education, and so forth. They started to look better and better to him. There was no war on, and maybe it wasn't a bad time to join the armed forces. They promised that they could teach you electronics and medical technology and lots of other things. Maybe that was just as good, if not better than going to college. He went to the recruiting office, came home one day, and told his mom that he had decided to join the navy. The navy recruiter had told him they would send him to electronics school and that he could learn to be a radar technician. Or maybe he would work on computers, or some other kind of high-tech activity, if he would sign up. The recruiter told him that was a promise and that by joining the navy, he could guarantee himself a new life.

He joined the navy and did learn electronics. He held them to their promise. Even though they tried to divert him into radio broadcasting and telegraphy school, he managed to make them stick to their promise, and he did learn electronics. In the bargain, he learned the ins and outs of radio sets. He became a technician in the navy, and eventually was pretty good. He learned how to use some of the computers and some of the complicated coding and decoding machinery. He finally was assigned overseas. He was sent to one of the big naval bases in Japan, and got to learn even more about the sophisticated machinery and electronic gear that they had there.

After his four-year enlistment was up, they asked him to re-enlist because he was so good at what he did. He felt, however, that now he had a really good skill and the beginning of a profession. This might be the break he had always looked for. He decided, instead of re-enlisting, to return home and maybe begin his own career in electronics.

Gary came back to the Palm Springs area and found that there was a need in the growing desert community for experts in these kinds of technical areas. The local hospital needed people who knew how to run their complicated computers. Hospitals nowadays have more electronic equipment than they do surgical equipment. They need computers to run their X-ray machines and their "CT scans." They need computers in their monitors on cardiac patients and, of course, all of their business equipment is run with computer assistance. Gary was 'just what the doctor ordered,' and he got a good job at the local hospital. He started to make pretty good money, and had a lot of fringe benefits. Things seemed to be going in his direction at last. He was twenty-five. He was a professional person. He had a good income, and he was a man of the world.

While working at the hospital, Gary met one of the nurses there who had been married before, too, but was now divorced. She was attractive and bright, and she was a "professional" too. They started to date, and liked each other a lot. She had two little boys of her own that she took care of with some financial assistance from her ex-husband. Gary thought that maybe they could take the place of his own little boy who had gone off with his mother to the Northwest and whom Gary hadn't seen since he was an infant. His own natural child had now moved to the state of Washington, and had been out of touch with Gary since he had joined the navy.

Gary got married to Grace, his second wife, and he thought he finally had it made. His mother was pleased. She agreed that it was time for him to get married and that he was now old enough to make that choice. She didn't totally agree with the notion of men getting married more than once, both because of her ex-husband's example and because she felt that marriages were made by God to last forever. She believed that if they broke, they shouldn't be remade by man.

Nevertheless, she went along with the second marriage, because Gary did need a strong woman behind him and because Grace seemed to be that kind of person.

Unfortunately, the second marriage really never got off the ground either. There were, again, conflicts in schedules. Grace had to work "shifts" from time to time. That is, she had to work sometimes from three to eleven p.m. on the nursing shift when Gary was at home. He had to stay with her two kids. Then she would come home and go to sleep, because she was exhausted. But Gary would have to get up at seven and go to his job, and this created dissension "just like the first marriage." He could see things were going to develop the way they had in the first marriage, and he began to be concerned that the result would be the same.

Gary kept thinking that maybe he had the same kind of curse on him that had been his father's lot. Afterall, his father had four or maybe five marriages. He wasn't sure, because he had lost track and didn't keep in touch with the old man.

In the meantime, Grace had his child, this time a little girl that they named Melody. They both really tried to make the marriage work. There was no question about that, and people later on all agreed. It seemed doomed, though, because Grace began to feel that Gary wasn't sure about what he wanted from her. She also thought he was probably too critical of her as well. She said he began to "get religion" and start preaching to her. She felt that he was making too many demands of her and that he wanted to have her become perfect "just like my mother."

Finally, when Gary insisted that she come "for counseling to a Christian therapist," Grace drew the line. She didn't think that someone else could tell her how to run her life or her marriage, whether he was religious or God-fearing, or "Jesus Christ himself." She became increasingly annoyed at Gary and at the marriage, and eventually it just started to fall apart.

By the time Melody was three years old, the second divorce took place.

Gary felt that he was a failure once again. All the old thoughts of being just like his father and being useless and botching things up, and everything that he remembered his mother had told him seemed to be coming true. He now had two children by two different women, and still no family. Maybe he wasn't meant to be married. Maybe he should just devote his life to his work. But Gary still had sexual needs and urges, and he couldn't completely ignore them.

While still married to Grace and working at the hospital, as he did, he had plenty of opportunities to meet young women. He met plenty of them, and they made a play for him. He was a good looking fellow, and he had a good job. The fact that he was married was not an impediment for many of the single young women who were looking for a mate. One of them was Norma Jean. Norma Jean was also a nurse, just like Grace. Norma Jean had been married a couple of times before, and both efforts had ended in failure. Pretty soon Gary and Norma Jean began to commiserate with each other. She told him that she understood how he felt, because she had the same kind of experience. It was very hard to find somebody who was reliable, steady and who was serious, the way they two were. It was less than a year before Gary was married for the third time.

His mother by now was scandalized at the repeated marriages. After all, Gary was her son and she loved him. She thought that maybe God would show him the way and, hopefully, things would work out for the best. Norma Jean seemed like a nice girl, although she was probably "a little fast," but then Gary was probably just like his father. He couldn't control some of his impulses, and the sexual ones were among those. Margaret later recalled that she always did have reservations about Norma Jean. But she probably blamed Gary more for falling into the trap again than she did Norma Jean. Norma Jean was a young woman who was looking for a man to live with and to take care of her. Even though she had a good profession of her own, she probably would have preferred to have Gary take care of things, set up a home and a family, and let her stay home with the kids.

Almost inevitably, it seems, they had another child. This was Gary's third. It was another girl whom they named Sue Anne.

Later, when Gary looked back at things, his third marriage turned out to be a replay of his second. If he were honest with himself, he reflected, it was probably the same as the first, too. He simply was not able to get close enough to Norma Jean. He didn't seem to be able to listen to her nor to understand her. She began to have other interests. It was pretty clear after about a year that Norma Jean was losing interest in Gary, both sexually and emotionally. He finally confronted her with the notion that she was still talking to and having too much to do with her last husband. They had only been divorced two years, and they had some children together. He knew that they saw each other from time to time.

Norma Jean denied this. But she didn't deny that she was interested in other men, and finally told Gary that the whole marriage was a mistake. She was sorry that they had the child, but she felt Gary wasn't the right man for her. He was too interested in work and in "heavy things" than he was in "living your life and having some fun for a change." He felt maybe she was right about this, but he didn't think he could change. So, they agreed to separate.

By this time, Gary had three children by three different wives. He was still supporting the second child by his second wife, as well as the third child by his third wife. They had made a separation agreement. He didn't ever see the first child, and had lost track of that boy altogether. All the efforts that he and Norma Jean had made at reconciliation seemed to be fruitless. They had gone to counseling and seen their pastor and even seen a psychologist. As in the second marriage, nothing seemed to work. Gary was becoming more and more despondent. He considered suicide.

On one occasion, his mother reported, he took a whole bunch of pills. She thought he was trying to kill himself then. They were mainly aspirin and some antihistamines, so the only thing that happened to Gary was the he got sick to his stomach and threw up most of the pills anyway. He later denied that he was trying to kill himself, but gave no good explanation to explain his behavior.

He began brooding, and used to sit alone in his apartment when he wasn't working. He had a .38 caliber revolver. He had bought it sometime earlier when Norma Jean was concerned about being home alone while he was at work. He had thought to give it to her so she would keep it in the house, and was going to teach her how to use it. Their troubles had come to a head by then, and he never got around to it. He looked at the gun from time to time, and checked it out. Once or twice, he thought about using it against himself. He knew this was against God's law, and knew that it would not be what he was supposed to do. So, he never tried that.

After about six months of separation, Gary became increasingly withdrawn. He had heard stories about Norma Jean dating some man who had been a friend of her second husband's. He began to wonder if actually she was living with this fellow in the house that he and Norma Jean had put a down payment on. This thought made him angry, especially since Norma Jean had their little girl with her. A toddler was certainly susceptible to bad influences. He didn't want her seeing this guy, whoever he was, embracing and kissing, touching and loving her mother when, he (Gary) was the rightful father. He decided that the best thing to do was to go to the house and check it out. He thought he better take the pistol with him (he later said). If Norma Jean were alone and the guy was not around, he could give it to her so she could take care of herself in case some bad fellow came around. He didn't say what he intended to do with it if he found the man there.

Although what he did do shortly became apparent.

He got into his car and drove to the home that he and Norma Jean had bought when they first got married. They were in the flush of their hopes and dreams for the future. It was a small tract-type house, the kind that was springing up all over the Coachella Valley. Many people who had originally come to Palm Springs and the surrounding resort cities in the forties and fifties had lived in weekend houses and places on golf courses. In recent years, however, a larger and larger middle class was springing up. There were tract houses going up all over the Valley, and they were within the price range of working people, especially when both couples had good jobs. Both Gary and Norma Jean thought this would be a good way to start their new family. Since they both were employed, it seemed reasonable to put a down payment on one of the houses.

The house had three bedrooms and a reasonable sized living room. There was a fairly good-sized yard in the back, and someday they hoped to put in a pool. Since pools are useful in Palm Springs for all year round, this is not an unusual thing for even a middle-class family to do. If you can afford to keep it heated, you can swim on Christmas and New Year's Day while watching television scenes of people back east spinning their wheels in the snow. Everyone in town loves this, and congratulate each other on being so smart to live there on these occasions.

It was late on a Sunday afternoon when Gary got to the house. There was no one around, and the doors were locked. The car was not in the driveway, and he felt that Norma Jean was out with the kids visiting. He thought he would do a little detective work, and he found a window near the bedroom which was usually left ajar. He pushed it open and climbed in. He started looking around the house to see if there was any evidence of some man living there. He didn't like what he found. There were some men's clothes in his closet. There were toilet articles belonging to some man, a razor and some after-shave lotion and shaving cream, and they were not his. He looked in some of the drawers and found some more clothing and underwear and socks. It quickly became clear to him that someone had indeed moved in. He even found some letters which apparently this fellow had written to Norma Jean. The man's name was Walter. He didn't sign the last name, but it really didn't matter. He was someone who had come in to destroy what was left of Gary's fantasy and dream.

Gary grew more and more angry, and as he was looking around, he heard the car pull up in the driveway. He felt that probably Norma Jean would be with the guy and also with little Sue Anne. He hid in the closet, not knowing what to do. As he stood in the closet, he heard them come in. There was indeed a man there and his estranged wife and their child, Sue Anne. He heard them all talking and laughing, and he got more and more angry and confused.

Finally, he heard Norma Jean talk to Sue Anne about taking a bath, and the water was being run in the tub. He despised the notion of seeing, in his mind's eye, some other man touching his baby. "This guy was probably going to give her a bath and act as if he were really the father." His rage grew, and he recalls blacking out. The only thing he remembers hearing was Sue Anne crying, "Daddy, daddy, daddy." He was sure she was calling for help and, in some way, demanding that he come to her rescue. He didn't know what the reason was for her cries nor what he had to save her from. He knew he had to do it, and he couldn't wait. He burst out of the closet, and had the gun in his hand.

He raced down the corridor from the bedroom to the bathroom, and there was this man standing in the way. All he could think of was he had to get him out of the way. The next thing he knew he heard the gun go off once and then twice, and the man fell. He ran into the bathroom to see Sue Anne standing by the tub. She was certainly screaming now. So was Norma Jean. Norma Jean saw the whole thing, and started screaming, "You killed him, you killed him," and turned and started running out of the house. For some reason, he started to chase her. He says that he remembers running after her out through the garage and into the driveway. He thinks he shot his gun at her again, he doesn't know.

The next thing he remembers is getting into his car and driving away. He thought possibly he had hurt the man badly. He didn't know if he had hit Norma Jean at all, he didn't think so. He started driving west, and was driving for about an hour trying to get his thoughts together. He remembers that he finally saw a Highway Patrol car on the freeway near one of the exits. He said that he pulled off and went over to the Highway Patrolman, and gave himself up.

The district attorney later had a somewhat different version of these events, even including Gary's surrender to the police. The D.A. said there was a dragnet out for Gary and that the Highway Patrolman actually had stopped Gary on the highway, recognizing the car, and arrested him. He also claimed that Gary had tried to tackle Norma Jean in the house and, having failed that, pursued her and fired three shots at her. Apparently, neighbors had heard the shots too, and thought he was trying to shoot her dead. The district attorney felt that this was in order to remove witnesses to the crime, and Norma Jean, of course, was the prime witness.

The district attorney said a lot of other things in court to try to prove that Gary had not benignly gone to his estranged wife's house to give her a gun. He believed that Gary had gone there with the specific purpose in mind of finding Norma Jean in a compromising situation. He speculated that, in fact, Gary had hid in the closet waiting for Norma Jean to come home with her new boyfriend. He suggested that Gary had the gun there for only one purpose, and that was to kill both Norma Jean and the boyfriend. He told the jury that he was certain that Gary had accomplished the first killing as he had intended, and just missed on carrying out a double murder. The D.A. thought that Gary probably then intended to steal the child and run away before anyone would know what had happened.

Gary's attorney, of course, denied this, and stuck to Gary's story which we have just recounted above.

After a somewhat lengthy trial, the jury chose to believe the district attorney, and convicted Gary of first-degree murder.

Later, because it was the contention of the district attorney, as well as Norma Jean, that the little child never cried, "Daddy, daddy" at all, there was some question in the mind of Gary's defense attorney as to whether or not Gary had hallucinated the whole thing. He wanted psychiatric input to see if Gary possibly could be the kind of person who had delusions and hallucinations. Perhaps he was not acting with reason and logic, but out of pressure from his internal stress and pressure.

It is necessary in California to present this kind of evidence before a jury too. That is, even after a jury convicts someone of a capital crime, such as murder, they also have to deliberate separately upon whether or not the killer is stable and competent and responsible for his crime. If he is not, and the jury judges that he is insane, then he is committed to the state hospital for the criminally insane until he is "cured." It is very rare that anyone is ever felt to be completely cured.

Therefore, many of these people stay in state prisons for much longer terms than they would have to serve had they been simply accused and convicted of murder without a plea of insanity. In this instance, however, the jury waived the evidence of the psychiatrist and psychologist, and felt that despite the indications that he might have been hallucinating and that he might have been laboring under a major delusion, he was still responsible for his act.

The real issue in understanding this and other crimes is not whether or not someone did it, but why they did it and how to prevent similar things from happening in the future.

It would seem that Gary Lomak killed a man whom he didn't even know. At the time of the trial, he didn't even know the man's name. He heard it on many occasions during the course of the courtroom scenes, but he actually never knew who it was he was shooting when he did so. The fact is that having been in the closet and only hearing the voice, he never actually saw this man until the moment he pulled the trigger and ended his life. It would really appear that what Gary was killing was not to him a real person, but an illusion. It was the man who had destroyed his marriage. It might have been the evil father who had botched up his whole life and had never done anything right. It might have even been part of himself who should be destroyed and done away with. These were some of the theories of the psychologists and psychiatrists who had tested Gary prior to the jury deliberation. They had testified in this direction in court.

While these ideas might be accurate, the real problem in these kinds of cases is that juries, like most of us, like to have things in black and white and clearly understandable. They are not happy with theories that allow people to "get off" of murders. They don't like the notion that someone might do something and not be responsible for it. It is very rare, even in California, for someone to get off on a "Twinkie" defense. This is the same as the case in San Francisco where a man was given a manslaughter alternative to the murder of two public officials because his attorney said he had been eating "Twinkies" and other sugary items and had had a temporary state of insanity. Whatever the reasons for the success of the Twinkie defense, I haven't seen it before nor since. It is unlikely, in my view, that it will ever be successfully pled in California again, and probably not anywhere else.

There are people who have delusions, and there are people who hallucinate. Whether or not we should hold them responsible personally for the disease which they have is a question that society has tried to solve for many years. It goes as far back as the famous McNaughton case. McNaughton was the name of a Scottish nobleman who was quite mad. He came to believe that Sir Robert Peale, the British Prime Minister in the middle of the nineteenth century, was personally trying to destroy him. Sr. Robert Peale had been responsible for passing some legislation known as the "Corn Acts." These had an unfavorable effect on this Scottish nobleman's fortunes, and he decided that Sir Robert Peale had done this in order to destroy McNaughton personally. McNaughton then decided that the only way to handle this was to come to London and go to Parliament and shoot Sir Robert Peale dead.

Lord McNaughton did in fact come to Parliament. He was armed, and he intended to kill Peale. He had never seen Sir Robert Peale, so when he got to the Houses of Parliament, he stopped someone who seemed to know what was going on there, and asked him if he would point Sir Robert Peale out to him. The members were leaving the Houses of Parliament at that time for their luncheon recess. As Sir Robert Peale emerged with his secretary, the person whom McNaughton had asked pointed the two of them out. McNaughton walked up to the secretary and shot him dead, thinking that he indeed was Sir Robert Peale.

McNaughton was immediately apprehended and confessed that he had killed Peale, because he knew that Peale was personally trying to destroy him, and that it was an act of self-defense. It turned out that it was not Peale, but a jury of his peers decided that McNaughton was not guilty by reason of his insanity. Actually, McNaughton was tried in the House of Lords, since he was a peer of the realm and was entitled to a jury of his peers. The Lords, in the House of Lords assembled, decided that someone who was so mad as not to understand the difference between right and wrong nor understand the consequences of his act was not guilty of premeditating and implementing a murder.

This rule still applies in many states in the United States, as marriages, he might still be married to number one, two or three. Perhaps if, as Norma Jean had suggested, he took more time to live his life fully and enjoy it, he wouldn't have ended someone else's. Perhaps if he and

107

any one of his three ex-wives had together gone for counseling and stuck to it until something could be worked out, some of these problems would have been avoided. So many lives could have been saved from ruin and one from death.

We cannot be sure of any of these. Perhaps the best we can do at this time is to try to counsel people when they start to get into difficult marital situations to try to use reason and logic in dealing with their problems. We have to try to help them to avoid impulsive acts of violence and rage. When they do feel them coming on, they must learn to back away. I have seen a number of cases, since the case of Gary Lomak, which could easily have ended in a similar kind of explosion. I think we were able to help avoid this kind of problem by pointing out the lessons to be learned in this murder and in others of a similar nature. Perhaps the concepts that can be learned from this case and from similar ones can avoid …

A NEW WORD FOR MURDER

CHAPTER 8

The Wages of Skin

Killers come in all sorts of varieties of shapes and forms, genders and races.

In our country most killers are ordinary people. They look like you and me, and they act much as we do. The core of the act of murder may be found in all of us. It's just that very few carry out the act itself.

When we were little kids, we used to play games like teasing each other and daring each other to do things. "I dare you to jump off that wall," and the brave and daring ones would take the dare and jump. Sometimes they would break a leg or maybe just a few fingers. "I dare you to cut school," and sometimes we would get caught by the truant officer, but other times get away with it.

Sometimes we could be teased into doing things and made to feel that if we don't, there is something wrong with us. Sometimes teasing can become more and more dangerous, both to the teaser and the one being teased. Some people can tease themselves to death.

When Arthur Mortensen called the Palm Springs Police and reported that his wife, Janice, had been missing for more than twenty-four hours, neighbors and friends were not terribly surprised. Janice, who was a twenty-nine-year-old legal secretary, had been known, as is common in small towns, to have "fooled around." Make no mistake about it, Palm Springs is a small town. Even though it is the glittering center of a necklace of bejeweled towns strung along the Coachella Valley and the focus for hundreds of thousands of tourists from all around the world, it still is a small town. When "the season" begins, sometime after the beginning of January, and people start flocking in from Kansas City and Milwaukee and Vancouver, as well as from New York and London, they are always seen as "the tourists." Even though they might have lived during the wintertime in the Valley for twenty or thirty years, they are not considered part of the permanent infrastructure of the Valley.

The real hard core of any resort town are the middle-class citizens who live there and who make it work, the doctors and lawyers, the accountants and political functionaries. This also, of course, includes the merchants and all of the employees of the above-named people.

Arthur and Janice Mortensen fit in with this middle-class infrastructure very nicely. Arthur was a thirty-seven-year-old furniture store owner, who had been quite successful in his ventures, selling upper class furniture to people who had come to "live the good life" in the Valley. They had usually sold their homes in Duluth or Rapid City lock, stock and barrel. They rarely wanted to move the middle-class, heavy "winter furniture" to Palm Springs. They wanted to get the brightly colored, gold and white stuff they saw in Arthur's store. Often, they were taken by white leather couches and gleaming crystal and chrome tables, which was something they had never even seen in Indianapolis, except when they went to the movies.

Arthur did an excellent business in his store, and was also branching out with several other places scattered around the Valley as well. He was thinking of setting himself up as an interior designer so that he could make the outrageous fees that these people commanded. Whether he did that or not, though, his furniture business was booming, and it was all due to his hard work and labor.

Arthur was born of a middle-class Swedish-American family in Minnesota. They had all shared the traditional values of hard work and energy which would bring success. Arthur remembers his father always saying, "If you do your work, you'll succeed."

His life story was really the classic example of the Protestant work ethic succeeding in America. His father was a Lutheran minister, in a small town in Minnesota, and his mother had raised the family in accordance with the values of her husband and of the church. They all had agreed that hard work and goals were essential to living the good life and to being wholesome. Arthur might have been considered monolithic in his adherence to these values.

Arthur went to high school, and even though he wasn't a great athlete, he knew that if he used his perseverance and energy he would succeed. He went out for track, and became a member of the long-distance team. He wasn't an Olympic class runner, but he survived, and he led his team to a number of inter-scholastic victories all over the north central region. He also became a member of the debate team. He was known to his teachers and fellow students as the most tenacious of debaters who would never give up. Arthur usually won out by sticking to his point and never yielding. Although he never became an "A" student, he did work hard. He remembered that this was the way to get success in life. He was advised by his counselors in high school to go into a business career where he could best apply his talents for hard work and perseverance and energetic pursuit of a goal.

Before doing this, however, Arthur decided to join the Air Force. In that way, not only could he get some experience and save some money, but also so that he could get government support to go to college through a program which the Air Force offered him in high school. He did this, as he did everything else, with energy and with goal-directed activity. In fact, he worked himself up in a series of clerical positions into a job of responsibility.

He was assigned to the Vandenberg Air Force Base in Central California, and became an important member of the team at the console directing the launching of rockets and space probes. He knew that this was due to his dedication to duty and to the fact that the officers and directors of the program knew that Arthur was the kind of man whom one could rely on not to make a mistake and not to panic under pressure.

While still in the Air Force, Arthur began taking courses in junior college. He was interested in a business career, and took courses in this direction.

He was interested in accounting and bookkeeping and a course called microeconomics. He studied hard and got good grades, and always maintained a "B" average. He decided finally that he would not like to make the Air Force a permanent career since he probably would have a lot of difficulty in becoming an officer. Besides that, he didn't feel that he should spend twenty or thirty years as a highly trained expert at any level without a chance to get an equity in the business. He knew that he could never have a piece of Vandenberg Air Force Base, except in the larger sense of being a citizen, and wanted to have his own thing. He decided that he would get a job in some business that looked promising to him in the retail area, and looked around for something to do after leaving the Air Force.

He found a small furniture store in Northern California that was looking for help, and he took a job there at night just before finishing up his enlistment. He decided that he liked the kind of work that the furniture business provided, and also the possibilities for expansion and big profits were intriguing to him.

It was while in the furniture business as an assistant manager that he met Janice. She was a pretty, dark-haired lady who seemed to enjoy life and who took a job in Arthur's store as a Christmas add-on helper. She was still a high school senior, and Arthur saw in her great possibilities. She was bright and quick and very pretty. She really got a kick out of life, and that was something Arthur realized he needed how to learn himself. He knew that while he had been keeping his nose strictly to the grindstone, he had missed something of the joy of life. All work and no play had made Arthur a dull young man. He was smart enough to know this, and figured that if he could allow some of Janice's "joi de vivre" to rub off on him, it would be to his benefit as well as to hers. He felt that he could teach her how to be a little more stable, and steady and how to make something of her life as well.

Janice had a similar kind of view, and felt that Arthur was probably her key to getting out of the small-town environment in which she found herself. She knew that there was a lot more in life than living in a small town and getting a job in a store. Her own family had done this kind of thing for a couple of generations, and it was not for her. Arthur was bright and energetic and, clearly, very ambitious. He didn't intend to stay in any kind of small town, and he fully expected to become a business tycoon commanding vast areas of empire in the commercial field. She had faith in Arthur, and he had plans for her.

They talked a lot and got to know each other. Arthur discovered that Janice, although she was still eighteen, had a lot to offer him in more ways than one. He had neglected his education in the area of sexuality, and Janice was an apt teacher. Arthur had been too busy working and studying, learning his Air Force rote, and his business courses to have much time left over for sex. It wasn't that he was not interested in it, it was just that he had different priorities. Janice's priorities were always different than Arthur's. She knew how to live and how to live to the fullest. Her friends told her she was probably going to burn the candle at both ends all through her life. She replied that it was probably better to let her candle burn brightly and shortly than to have a dull, sputtering flame go on for years and years. She was certainly prophetic in this regard.

Janice told Arthur a lot about sex, and she did it openly and freely. She wasn't ashamed of her sexuality nor of her interest in sex. Not only did she tell him, but she showed him. This was a problem for him at first, because he was used to the rather rigid doctrines which he had learned as a child from his father and mother. This wild California girl was something that he didn't quite know how to handle. He told her that he thought the only way for them to really feel comfortable, or at least for him to feel that way, was to get married. Janice, knowing that she probably had a good thing, agreed that this seemed like a reasonable proposition, and even though she was just finishing high school, she thought she would give it a try. When she explained this to Arthur, he was somewhat shocked, but felt he could change her to his way of thinking. That is, he believed that marriage wasn't just something "to give a try," but to devote one's life to, and to build a base for a family and a solid long-term relationship. He tried all the time to explain this to her. At first, she seemed to understand, although as time went on, it appeared that this was, as in many things with Janice, a superficial facade.

Arthur later told people that "Janice was just like an iceberg." Not that she was ever cold, far from it, but the portion of her that appeared on the surface was only about twenty percent of what was really going on underneath. She had a lot happening inside of her, and she wasn't all that she seemed to be.

Aside from everything else, Janice was bright. She kept encouraging Arthur in his business enterprises. After a couple of years when it appeared that he really had learned the business well, and when he talked to her about going out on his own and expanding, she encouraged him. She even helped by working. She had followed his advice and took training as a legal secretary. Legal secretaries do very well in California, as they do in most states, and she was actually bringing in more cash than. Arthur was when he was the manager of the local furniture store. She knew, however, that this was just "seed money," as he did, and they used both her and his incomes to save up enough to look around for a place of their own in a growing area. They had been to "the Springs" on one or two occasions on summer vacations.

The summertime is the time when people of less affluent means are able to come to Palm Springs and enjoy the same facilities that their wealthier brethren do in the winter. Hotel rates are extremely low, because the hotels would prefer to stay open all year round even if they only break even, then to close up and lose their reliable help. In closing, they also run the risk of having their machinery run down and their fountains dry up in the desert heat. Even when closed, they have to keep the air-conditioning on twenty-four hours a day to preserve things like furniture and wall hangings, and the like. Otherwise, they dry out, the glue cracks, and the wood splinters from the overwhelming heat and total dehydration of the one hundred-twenty-five degrees of the summers. It was, therefore, common practice for the hotels to offer rates at twenty-five percent of their winter rates, or even less, just to stay open. Arthur and Janice knew a good thing when they saw it. So, they came to Palm Springs and stayed for a few days to enjoy the illusion of living like millionaires on the income of a furniture store manager and a legal secretary.

While in "the Springs," Arthur and Janice also began to notice that it was a growing community. Afterall, it was part of the "sun belt." Most of the population of the United States seemed to be moving into that area of longer hours of sunshine and more warmth year-round. While Palm Springs certainly is an exaggeration of the "sun belt" to the utmost degree, it, in many ways, is the epitome of it. It is the place where the sun spends the winter, or so the Chamber of Commerce says. The fact that the sun also stays around during the summer and desiccates everything in sight can be handled with modern equipment.

What Arthur and Janice did is what most of the tourists do when they come to "the Springs." That is, they stay inside during the overwhelming heat of mid- day in their air-conditioned room and nap or play cards, or make love. After the mid-day heat is dissipated, they can either go out to the pool and soak themselves, or play tennis or golf or, of course, spend the evenings at the poolside. The incredible warmth of the desert does not stay on once the sun sets. Although it is ninety degrees often during the early evenings in the summer, the humidity is five percent, or less and, therefore, it doesn't seem very hot. Afterall, it is lower than body temperature, and by repeated dipping yourself into one of the ubiquitous pools all over town, you can allow the water to slowly evaporate and feel cool and comfortable all evening long.

They realized that they had found not only a growing community, but an area of exceptional opportunity. The community was growing, and the kind of growth that it offered was especially attractive to an ambitious couple. The people who would move to Palm Springs in the winter season were invariably well off, and brought with them large sums of money. They had sold their homes, usually for cash. For tax reasons, they needed to buy others of equal value. They also had to "keep up with the Joneses" and had to get furnishings equivalent to what they saw around them. They never intended to bring their "old stuff" from the mid-west or back east, so were furniture buyers "par excellence."

Arthur found a man who was interested in selling his own furniture store.

The store owner felt that he was getting worn out and worn down, and was reaching an age where he himself wanted to leave the business. Arthur made him an offer he couldn't very well refuse. He offered to give him a modest down payment, but a large percentage of his income for the next ten years if he turned the business over to him. Arthur had a good track record. The man knew that he was never going to get a better deal from any of the major chains that might be interested in taking over his business. He saw an opportunity to have an energetic and vigorous young man make a living for him while he enjoyed the declining years of his life in the Palm Springs sun.

Things went very well for Arthur in terms of his business. His marriage seemed to be okay, too, because he and Janice had two children, both boys. This was the foundation of what Arthur envisioned as the dynasty which he wished to create in the desert.

Janice, while giving birth to the children, informed Arthur at an early time that she had no intention of becoming a drab and dowdy housewife. She intended to keep her looks and never allow any middle-age spread. She went to health clubs and fitness clubs all of the time. She was back in her health club a month after the birth of each child. She maintained her figure, and was terrified that she would ever get stretch marks from pregnancy.

After she had the two boys, Janice informed Arthur that that was the end of child-bearing for her. He wanted to try again, at least one more time to have a girl, but she absolutely refused. He figured that he had better leave well enough alone, and quit while he was ahead. They agreed to quit reproducing, and raise the children as best they could. Janice said it would probably even be better if she went back to work as a legal secretary. Since she was able to make a very good cash income and since help was available to raise the children, they made their deal. Included in the deal was that Janice would be able to work as a freelance legal secretary and take care of her children as often as she could. For the rest of the time, they would bring in permanent help to the house. With Arthur's business, she seemed to feel this was a reasonable compromise.

The only problem was that Janice began meeting lots of different people in her work. There were an awfully lot of interesting attorneys around the Coachella Valley. Not only were there district attorneys, D. A. assistants and public defender deputies, but also all kinds of young aspiring attorneys, their clients and, every once in a while, a very cute policeman. It was the lawyers who attracted her the most, because they tended to be glib and snappy and very bright. Arthur was anything but dull in terms of business, but he never did develop a really good knack for talking the kind of cocktail chatter that Janice thought was fascinating. She began telling him about how clever and how cute this or that lawyer was, and he was starting to become concerned.

Finally, when Janice started to come in later and later at night, telling him that she had to take this deposition or that, or that she had to stay extra hours to type up her work, he became increasingly suspicious.

Of course, it is the husband who is the last to know. If Arthur had asked his neighbors or some of his friends in the business world, some of the members of the Rotary Club, or even a couple of attorneys who had befriended them, he would have known that "the cat was out of the bag" a long time ago. Janice was known as "an easy lay." She was the kind of girl who had "hinges on her heels." She was able to easily be carried away by the sparkling eyes of a young attorney, the brilliant smile of a court reporter and, even some said, "the big gun" of a deputy sheriff.

Finally, Arthur confronted her with his growing uneasiness about her hours and her activities and, as was consistent with her, she didn't deny it. She told Arthur that, after all, she had always been much more hedonistic than he.

Furthermore, she didn't see anything wrong with having a little fun on the side, especially since he was so dull and serious about everything, including having sex and children, and the like. She felt that he was only interested in building his empire and his own career. He never really wanted her to have fun or enjoy life. They argued about this often, and Arthur became increasingly scandalized and enraged. He kept pointing out to Janice that she was becoming an evil, sinful and scarlet woman. He was never that overwhelmingly religious, but he could think of no other way to talk to her about what he felt was her increasing disregard for the values of society and the core of our American way of life, as he put it.

On one or two occasions when Janice came in extremely late at night, screeching the tires of her new Firebird at three a.m., their arguments became loud and raucous. The girl they had staying with them to help take care of the kids later recalled that the arguments would become loud and violent. Occasionally, she believed that they had come to blows. The next day, either Arthur would have a scratch on his cheek or his chin, or possibly gingerly move his arm and hand. On one occasion, Janice had a lot of makeup on her face, and was wearing sunglasses early in the morning on a cloudy day. It didn't take a great detective to realize that things had gotten out of control from time to time between them.

It was not, therefore, a big surprise when Arthur called the police and said finally that Janice hadn't come home one night. He reported that she had been out in her new Firebird, probably running around with some detective or deputy sheriff, or maybe one of the deputy D. A.'s, and had decided not to return. He couldn't be sure. Maybe she had picked up some guy at one of the discoes in town. She liked to go to the discoes and allow herself to be picked up, so she could prove she was still an attractive young woman. Afterall, she was only twenty-nine and had, the figure of a nineteen-year-old. She kept pointing that out to Arthur, and he never denied it, nor did any of her male friends.

Arthur told some of this to the investigating police officer when he finally came around to check on the story that Janice was missing. She simply had not come home that night, and her car was not in the driveway. The officer took the story down, and then talked to some of the neighbors They, of course, told him some of the pertinent facts about Janice's social life and nocturnal habits.

The detective decided to try first by checking out the parking lots of the discoes in town and looking for the Firebird. Afterall, if she had gone off with some young man, she might well have left the car there, although everyone swore that it had almost become a part of her.

Sure enough, the Firebird was in the parking lot of one of the discoes, and apparently had been there all night and all the next day too. The parking lot attendant noticed it when he came in to work the next morning, and said it had been there when he left his job at midnight. He always left at midnight, and many of his customers still had their cars parked there. He had other things to do, so he missed a few tips from the patrons who wanted their cars after twelve o'clock.

There were not that many of them, but he does remember that the Firebird was there when he left. It was setting there locked when he came back on the second day and the detective came around to check out the missing person story. There were no keys in the car, although the attendants usually left the keys under the floor mats of the late-returning patrons. The parking lot man noticed this, and said that regulars knew about this, and she probably had taken the keys and gone off in someone else's car, locking her own for safety.

Since Janice had been so attached to her car, the detective began to wonder why she took the risk of leaving it alone in a lot even though she may have had the keys. He started questioning more people around town who might have known her. He went to a number of her regular employers who were attorneys known to him. They told him more about Janice's way of life and her activities, and also hinted that Janice and Arthur were not always very happy, and especially lately had been at odds an awful lot. One of them pointed out that Janice had come in to work a few weeks ago with "a big mouse under her eye." When he had joked with her about it, she didn't banter back with her usual quips and wisecracks. He realized it was something serious, and backed away. He began to think that possibly Arthur was not being as quiet and passive as he had been before. Maybe he had finally begun to understand what Janice was up to. In any event, he told the detective something about their backgrounds. More and more people confirmed these stories.

When an all-points bulletin failed to reveal any sign of Janice, and when she made no effort to contact her children after three days, the search was intensified. It became clear that Janice was truly missing and not just off on a weekend lark with some casual lover. Despite all of her sexual excesses, she had always loved the children, been close to them, and had always come home to them before.

Janice had told her girlfriends that if she and Arthur ever broke up, she would make sure that she had the children in her custody. This was to ensure that he wouldn't "make them into clones of himself." She felt that the children should have the ability to choose their own kinds of lives and enjoy life as much as they could. She was convinced that her presence in the family was necessary to balance out Arthur's monolithic drive towards success and achievement. Janice was no dummy. She had achieved a lot in her life with a minimum of education.

Although her values concerning sexual morality were different than Arthur's, she was at least his equal in intellectual capacity.

It became clear that, for some reason, her absence was a much more ominous sign of foul play than Arthur had indicated. The police began to suspect that he had something to do with it. They talked to him on several occasions. He said that he simply didn't know what had happened to her. The detective also talked to the house girl who had been staying with the children most of the time, and working for the Mortensen's for the past two years. She said that as far as she knew, she went to sleep at eleven or twelve o'clock on the night of Janice's disappearance. She thought she heard Janice's car pull up at two or three in the morning, but couldn't be sure. She heard some noises and a thumping kind of sound in the bedroom, but never did get up to investigate. Since the sounds did not continue and she was used to hearing a lot of noises in that house anyway, she stayed in her room. She told the police something about the couple's previous arguments. She thought that there had possibly been one that night, but she couldn't be sure. She had stayed in bed, and went back to sleep. She doesn't know if it had even been Janice's Firebird that had crunched up the gravel of the driveway at three in the morning. It could well have been Mr. Mortensen's car too. He had told her the next day that he had gone out looking for Janice when she didn't return at midnight and that he had come back about two or three in the morning. So, it easily could have been him too, she just didn't know. The police were more suspicious.

Eventually, they began checking out other possibilities, and discovered that the Mortensen's had a summertime retreat. After Arthur had started to make some decent income in the furniture store, they were able to use Janice's money to buy a summer place. The Coachella Valley is surrounded by high mountains which, in fact, give it its unique climate both winter and summer. The mountains offer a haven from the summer heat of the desert floor. The Indians, who first inhabited the region, used to commute regularly up to the slopes of the San Jacinto Mountains in the summertime, leaving the Valley at the beginning of June, and only returning late September. A number of the local residents had learned of this trick, and had bought summer vacation lodges on the surrounding mountainsides.

Idyllwild is a community about seven thousand feet up, which, if taken in isolation, appears to be a town somewhere in the Green Mountains of Vermont. It is filled with pine trees and the scent of pine. It is a lush deep green all of the time, being sprinkled with large amounts of Pacific moisture, as the incoming clouds off the Pacific Ocean are stopped by the coastal range of mountains and release all of their rain on the western slopes of the San Jacinto and sister mountains. This is what makes the desert on the other side of the mountains so dry. The clouds never have a chance to reach the desert to the east, as they discharge all of their moisture on the western slopes, thereby, making Idyllwild and environs at high elevations very much like Vermont and New Hampshire. The local residents from Palm Springs have summer homes there and, of course, the hardy mountaineers at Idyllwild stay year-round and literally enjoy a winter wonderland in December and January.

As a result, the Palm Springs area is a picture postcard scene in the winter months, a palm studded oasis surrounded by majestic snow-capped mountains. Arthur and Janice spent a good deal of the summertime in the mountain cabin, but very little time there in the winter. Since it was early spring, it was still rather cold on the mountainside, and very muddy.

The detectives thought it might be a good idea to go to the cabin in Idyllwild and look around. They, of course, needed a search warrant. In view of the fact that the Mortensen's had been known to have been bickering and fighting and had even come to blows on at least one occasion, there was not much trouble in getting a judge to sign a warrant. Janice had been missing for more than three days, and the warrant was executed.

The detectives went to the cabin in Idyllwild and looked around inside of it.

It seemed to be, as Arthur had told them, in perfect order. Most things that Arthur did were in perfect order anyway. The furniture was neat and clean. It had dust covers on it, and the doors were locked tight. There was no evidence that anyone had been there in several weeks or months. The ground around the cabin was very muddy and slushy, and one of the detectives noticed, as he looked in the back, that there was an old wooden door lying on the lot of the adjoining property. This wasn't the property where Arthur and Janice lived, but was right on the other side of an electric power line. He wondered why a wooden door would be lying out there in the middle of an unoccupied lot. He also wondered why it wasn't quite as weather beaten as he thought it should have been after having been covered with snow and then having the snow melt. It didn't show any signs of water spots or dirt accumulation. He walked over through the mud and looked at it. When he picked it up, it looked very much to him as though the earth underneath it had been disturbed quite a bit. In fact, it looked like it had been spaded up. Even in the mud it looked like there were indications that the earth had been turned over and that the door had been placed there on purpose.

The detective had to call down to the county seat to get another search warrant since this was someone else's property. An invalid search warrant could make any evidence useless even if it was turned up. Something did turn up when the warrant arrived. It was Janice's body that was turned up. She was buried about two feet under the mud, wrapped in a carpet that appeared to be from Arthur's store. The top of Janice's head had been caved in with what the coroner described as "a blunt instrument, with severe force." The coroner felt she had been subjected to several heavy blows to the top and side of her head, and commented that "death resulted from the second or third blow, which fractured the temporal bone on the left side, piercing the cerebrum and causing a massive hemorrhage of the left cerebral artery." Apparently, there were four or five more blows which followed that, as the assailant wasn't sure that the victim was dead, and wanted to do a complete job.

Arthur was later arrested and charged with the murder of his wife. He denied that he was responsible at all. He said it was probably one of her boyfriends who got angry with her and finally did her in.

Later, when a search warrant was obtained for his Cadillac El Dorado, there was evidence of hairs from the rug which the body was wrapped in found in the trunk of the car. There was also a microscopic bit of blood which matched Janice's type and not Arthur's.

It wasn't one of the world's great detective mysteries, but it did indicate attention to detail and following up on leads. The district attorney asked the jury to come in with a verdict of first-degree murder.

Arthur's attorney entered a plea of not guilty in the initial hearings. A magistrate, however, bound the case over for trial in Superior Court, feeling that there was sufficient evidence to go ahead with a murder prosecution.

The district attorney eventually presented the case to a jury, and suggested 'that Arthur had become increasingly enraged with his wife's sexual acting out, and had planned to kill her as punishment for betraying him. He suggested that Arthur had gone out on the evening of the murder to look for his wife, but being unsuccessful in his search, returned home. He then proposed that the noise the house girl heard at three a.m. was indeed Janice's Firebird returning to its perch, and the thud was the struggle that Arthur and Janice had after their final argument. He asked them to believe that Arthur was waiting with the lethal weapon in his hand, which he also proposed was a hammer taken from Arthur's tool box. He further suggested to the jury that Arthur, having killed his wife, then wrapped her body in a piece of carpeting from his store, which he had previously brought home for that very purpose. He then told the jury that Arthur took the body, in the trunk of his car, to the side of the mountain and buried it in the wee hours of the night in a shallow grave near their weekend retreat. In his haste to cover up the evidence of the digging, he had covered the graveside with a wooden door which had been leaning against the side of his house under the eaves, where it had been protected from the weather. It was this lack of weather- beaten appearance that had given away the site to the detectives.

Later, Arthur, according to the D. A., returned home and drove Janice's Firebird back to the parking lot of the disco where she had told him she had been prior to the fight. He had parked it in the lot, hoping the attendant wouldn't notice the difference between where it might have been and where it was finally left. He was apparently successful in this regard. He then had taken the keys and had thrown them in the desert or in a sewer, as they had never been found.

Arthur's attorney tried to counter each of these arguments with a logical alternative. He suggested that Arthur had nothing to do with the crime at all. He felt that the evidence of the rug fibers in his car could easily have been due to the fact that Arthur moved material from his store and warehouse home, back and forth to different locations. He used the trunk of his car for valuable property, and the fibers certainly could have arrived in the trunk in that fashion. Also, it was quite possible that Janice had nicked her finger or cut herself in some way during the year or two that they had owned the El Dorado. There was no way of telling how old the blood spot was in the back of the car. The fact that the body was discovered in the lot near the weekend retreat was explained by the attorney as possibly being the place where Janice had taken her boyfriend for the night.

Perhaps they had gotten into a violent argument, and she had been brutally beaten to death, buried next door, with the unknown boyfriend escaping scot-free.

Despite the possibility of the defense attorney's arguments, the jury felt the overwhelming mass of evidence leaned more in the direction of Arthur's culpability. At the same time, they could not believe that he had planned, premeditated and carried out the killing in cold blood. As many juries do, they opted for a compromise. They decided, in their own wisdom, that Janice had indeed been promiscuous and had gone beyond the bounds of middle-class reason with her activities. They believed that Arthur had been provoked beyond what an ordinary man could handle, that while his behavior was reprehensible, it was understandable.

They returned with a verdict of voluntary manslaughter. This means actually that they believed the crime was committed with the knowledge and volition of the killer. At the same time, though, it was not done with malice and forethought, nor premeditation, nor specific intent to kill prior to the episode. In effect, they said it was a crime of passion.

Arthur was given a sentence of eight to twelve years in state penitentiary, with the possibility of parole after three. Since he had been an exemplary citizen, it was considered highly likely that he would indeed receive parole after three years, and try to go back and pick up the pieces of his life.

This is not an unusual crime, whether it be in Palm Springs or Palm Beach, Atlantic City or Albuquerque. The idea of extreme emotional stress causing someone to act beyond reason and beyond what they would ordinarily do in the course of everyday life has been accepted by the law for many years. The notion of provoking someone beyond his limits is a well-accepted tradition in Anglo- Saxon law, as it is in western culture in general. The amazing thing, in my experience, is that it is not done more often. I have frequently seen a number of situations in which wives will come in for psychiatric intervention after having become involved in love affairs with friends, neighbors and business associates. They are terrified lest their husbands discover what has happened and cause a violent and irreversible scene. Of course, the fact that they have the judgment and good sense to come in for intervention before something happens usually averts the episode in the first place.

A man who is used to order and reason in his life has great difficulty in living with and understanding someone of an opposite disposition. While it is true that opposites attract and that people with different personalities frequently complement one another, rather than detract from one another, there is a limit to this kind of polar difference. That is, complete opposites and people with absolutely differing points of view have difficulty reconciling these points of view. A man who is raised in a religious tradition with the values of home, family, hard work, church and fidelity as part of his credo can have overwhelming difficulty in living with and understanding a young woman whose values are related to sensual love, physical warmth, pleasure and a constant focusing on the briefness of life.

In Janice's case, the notion that life was brief and that one should live it to its hilt was a self-fulfilling prophesy. The intensity of her drive to enjoy every moment of her life and the overwhelming drive which forced her to live out these feelings ultimately was the cause and the seed of her own destruction. Arthur's values could not co-exist with Janice's. Probably, they should have been divorced several years before they finally parted company. But instead, this story is just ...

A NEW WORD FOR MURDER

CHAPTER 9

The Sex Queen Kills

Most kids start out when they are little playing games of all sorts. They play house and they play cowboys and Indians, and often they play cops and robbers. Usually, the desired role is that of the cops. Not too many of us want to be the robber or the bad guy. It is very rare that a kid growing up will decide that he or she wants to be seen as the killer or the kidnapper or the robber in these games that we all play. But within all these games, again, you find the seeds which can grow into the flower of death.

The cowboys that chase the Indians sometimes get ambushed and killed.

Usually, the Indians are massacred in some shoot out. Sometimes the cowboys kill each other in a "quick draw" contest. Even in the games of childhood, we read about these things in our daily papers or see the stories on the nightly news of one child shooting another in "a game."

As we grow older the games that we play take a different turn. Adolescents are preoccupied with sex, and sometimes "the dating game" becomes an obsession and an ever-present reality to teenagers. They fall in love and they have heart-rendering separations. Their whole lives are colored by their feelings of romance and magic. Once in a while the sexual passions become overwhelming and they themselves lead to games which get all mixed up. In the mix up of the games we can find the bright red thread peeping through, if we look carefully.

126

Carla Diana decided that she really ought to have two first names when she created her stage name. She had thought it out very carefully, and figured it would be more memorable that way. She felt in show business you had to create an image, and to have two first names probably would give her more class. Class was something Carla had always sought for, dreamed about, and rarely achieved. She believed her real name had no "class." Her real name actually was Clara Diane Vandermeel. She was from a Dutch family who lived in Grand Rapids, Michigan.

There are a lot of Dutch families in Grand Rapids. They had come over along with the tulip bulbs from Holland to Michigan, and later migrated to Grand Rapids, and worked in the furniture factories. Some of the families had worked in the farms nearby. There are a lot of truck farms around Grand Rapids. And Carla's family had originally come there to work them.

Carla figured that by taking her real name of Clara and transposing the letters to Carla, she would create something unique and memorable. She also thought that using her middle name Vandermeel sounds too much like wooden shoes and windmills, and it was too long anyway. All she did with her last name was to change Diane to Diana, and thought that everybody would remember her. As it turned out, they did.

Carla thought that class was really the main and most important thing in life. Her family never had any. Her father had worked for a produce distributor in Grand Rapids. He packed and dispatched fruit and vegetables all over the Midwest. He was a hard worker, and everyone thought he was "kind of quiet." He was quiet. He didn't have much to say. He stayed home and minded his own business. So did Carla's mother. She stayed home to take care of the three kids they had together. That was quite a job in itself.

In order to get some extra money, Mrs. Vandermeel began taking jobs around town cleaning houses "for the rich people." Carla knew that these rich people "had some class." They had nice furniture and expensive rugs, and beautiful pictures on the walls, that must have cost a small fortune. The houses were big with lots of rooms, and there were separate bedrooms for each kid, if there were any kids. There were gardens and big cars, and lots of clothes. There were furs and jewelry, and everything that went with them. That was what she wanted for herself. The biggest fear she ever had in her life was to wind up like her mother, "an old lady scrubbing other people's floors." She decided to get out of Grand Rapids as soon as possible.

When Carla was only sixteen when she married a soldier. She left home with him, and went off to live near an army camp. She got him to marry her because she told him she was pregnant. Actually, she wasn't pregnant at the time, but later he took care of that, and she did have a baby with him so he would not feel cheated.

By the time Carla had the child, he was away in Germany, and she had to come back home with her little girl for a while. He probably never forgave her for lying about the baby and, in the long run, the marriage never worked out. He came back and was mean to her. He drank a lot. He told her she was cheating on him while he was away. She said that never really was true, but he made her feel that it was. She finally decided "if you have the name, you might as well play the game." Carla was filled with all kinds of aphorisms and wise sayings like that.

She was sixteen when she got married and nineteen when she got her divorce. She had a two-year-old child, no special skill, and very little education, but she had a need. She had a need to have class. That overrode everything. She knew that the only way she could "break into class" was by going to New York City. She filed divorce papers, left her husband, and went with her child to New York. She thought that maybe she would look for a job as a model. That was not a bad idea, because Carla was in fact a beautiful woman.

Years later, after Carla got into all the trouble, which is the ultimate subject of this story, she was remembered by an acquaintance at a cocktail party. He had been a casting director in Hollywood for many years, and said that he remembered her trying out for a casting call in one of his big films. He said, "I'll never forget her. She was the most strikingly beautiful girl I ever saw. If she only had any talent, she could have gone far."

That was probably Carla's greatest blessing and greatest curse. She had beauty, but not much more to go with it. She was extremely well proportioned. She had average heigh and was slim, but adequately endowed by her creator with curves "in the right places," as she put it. She did her best to be striking and attention-getting. She was really blonde, just like a little Dutch girl in the ads. But she decided that she would be more striking by dying her hair jet black. With her jet-black hair and her extremely fair, almost white skin and blue eyes, she did make an appearance which one could not easily forget.

She was sort of like an Aubrey Beardsley black and white pen and ink drawing. To further the illusion, she always tried to wear only black and white clothing. This was sort of like the movies of the thirties in which all of the main characters are dressed in either black or white, or silver and gray, or variations of these themes. She had spent a lot of time at the movies, and paid especial attention to the films of the thirties and early forties, because they "reeked with class." She had dyed her hair jet black and wore it in a page-boy style, hanging down to her shoulders and slightly curling there, "just like Joan Bennett." She thought maybe she looked like Joan Bennett, and maybe she did.

In any event, Carla did get some jobs. Men liked her, and they liked to look at her. She hoped to make it in show business and in modeling, and maybe, every once in a while, she had to go out of her way to please the men who gave out the jobs. She thought this was part of the business. Afterall, in one of her favorite aphorisms, "It isn't what you know, it's who you know." And she got to know an awful lot of people. They were mostly marginal men in the sleezy borderland of show business and modeling where "an actress was somebody who could act the right way at the right time for the right people." She never did really get any major parts, although she appeared in a number of "reviews." These were shows that appeared in local burlesque theaters in New York and New Jersey, and then would occasionally travel up to Boston or down to Wilmington, Philadelphia, or points west. This really was not the kind of work that Carla wanted to do, and it didn't have much class either. She thought she was running into some kind of dead end, and figured that maybe the thing to do was to more carefully choose a mate, not for the purpose of getting away from home this time, but for the purpose of "making it in the business."

Her second husband was a photographer. He had taken a number of pictures of Carla, which he had sold to a variety of second-rate "men's magazines" over the years. She was ideally suited for these magazines. Her striking beauty and her willingness to pose in whatever attire or lack of it was required by the magazine made her suitable for their "photographic essays."

Her second husband's name was Al. He had worked in photography around the metropolitan New York area for most of his life. He was about twice Carla's age. When he married her; he was forty, she was twenty-one. The marriage did not last very long, because Carla felt he was "a queer." He rarely was able to satisfy her sexually, and she believed he was using her "as a front." She pointed out that all of the men she knew "used me."

Being used by men was something she had become accustomed to. It became questionable whether she was doing the using or being used. In any event, her attempt to marry her way upwards into class had not worked out. Al was not really able to make much headway for her. He didn't have any significant contacts, and he didn't get her much more work than she had had before she married him. He wasn't really interested in her little girl, nor in raising her. He didn't make a great deal of money, and he wasn't able to put her up in the kind of style she had hoped for in Manhattan. She had always dreamed of having an apartment facing the East River with a view of the Queensborough Bridge. She saw that in lots of the movies with Madeline Carrol and William Powell and Joan Bennett and all the other stars she admired.

It wasn't so hard to file for divorce the second time. She found a lawyer in Manhattan who had represented a couple of the "shows" she had worked with, and he helped her to get the divorce. In those days it wasn't as easy to get a divorce as now, but Al didn't argue much, and they were able to file on the basis of adultery. She later thought that maybe Al was pleased by this legal nicety. "It gave him a reputation which he didn't deserve," she said, bitterly. Nevertheless,

Al agreed to be the guilty party and allow her to file against him, and the divorce was granted.

Carla met husband number three, Willy, through her lawyer. Willy produced the kinds of shows she had worked in before. But at least he was the producer. He put on small shows in hotels and resorts in the Catskill Mountains. These were not really Broadway productions, but they were actual shows, and people got paid for them. Willy made a good living. She was twenty-three when she married Willy after her unsuccessful attempt with Al, and by now her little girl was six.

Willy kept promising to give Carla "a good part" in one of his shows. Of course, he did not have many good parts or many parts of any kind to give away. Carla wasn't able to sing, and she couldn't dance very much either. She was able to be the "straight man" for a couple of comedians in their shows. She developed a reputation for being "a Borscht Belt Gracey Allen." She would play the dumb, but attractive young girl against the comic in the various hotels on the Borscht Circuit. Most of the routines were stolen from Burns and Allen or other successful "big time" acts, but that didn't matter to Carla. She had seen most of them anyway on T.V. What really mattered to her was making it into the big time and getting some "class." This wasn't to be had in the Borscht Circuit. She could see that this effort wasn't making her get where she wanted to go either. Besides that, Willy started "using me again."

Willy's career was mired down in the Borscht Belt too. He began to think that he could possibly get a break if only he had the right contacts in the upper echelons of show business. He needed some more clout with "the big boys on Broadway." He began asking Carla if she would do him a favor from time to time. The favor, of course, was to "be nice to some of the boys." Carla knew what being nice meant. She had been nice to people for several years now, and it hadn't gotten her very far. Nevertheless, this was one area in Carla's education which did not need post-graduate training. She knew how to be nice and extra nice.

Unfortunately, it didn't get her anywhere, and it didn't work for Willy either.

Carla realized after a couple of years of the marriage that she was at another dead end. She didn't have any special talent for show business. She was not really a great actress, and Willy didn't know how to be a successful producer.

She began to see him as a loser, and decided if she stuck with him "I'd sink along with him with all flags flying." So, she got out of that marriage too.

If nothing else, Carla was persistent. She was almost obsessed now with the notion of making it and having class. Realizing that she had created a somewhat negative image in New York City, she decided to head west. She left for California and Hollywood. She was still in her mid-twenties and still extremely attractive.

She had some names and some contacts of agents, a few actors and producers in L. A. Carla thought maybe she could get some work in films.

By now, she had decided that getting work in films was really only going to be the stepping stone to meeting the right kind of man. At this point, even Carla recognized that her talents were somewhat minimal and her major assets were her good looks and her body. She did meet an agent, and he started to get her some work. She got jobs in a number of small films and even some small parts in big films.

"Maybe you saw me in 'The Lonesome Cowboy'? I played a cowgirl there.

There were some big names in that picture. Did you see 'The Steel Jungle'? Or how about 'The Ancient Monster'? I had a speaking line in that one."

Most of the films were very forgettable, and most of her roles in them even more so. But she made a living, and her daughter was growing up, and she clung to her hope.

She had an apartment in the Hollywood Hills, and life wasn't too bad, but she always needed a little bit more money.

Husband number four was a Filipino film technician. He had come to California to work on some films, and wanted desperately to stay in this country. There is a small quota on Orientals emigrating to the United States, and one way to get around that is to marry an American citizen. It does not automatically make you a citizen any longer, as it did in the old days, but at least it allows you to get a visa so that you can stay in this country. You can get a green card and work as a resident alien, and eventually file for citizenship. "It was a marriage of convenience, that is, his convenience, not mine. He used me too. He married me so he could stay in the country. He promised to give me a new car and also to introduce me to some of the higher-ups in the movie business that he knew through his work as a technician. I didn't get the car, and the only other people I met were some more Flips like him. I guess I could have been the queen of the movies in Manila, but he didn't even want to do that. He wanted to stay in L. A., so we agreed to get a divorce after a year or two, I forget how long it lasted."

After that, Carla's film career started to change. It wouldn't be fair to say that it declined, because she started to get more featured roles. Unfortunately, the features were in films that were not seen in most movie theaters. In the old days, they used to be shown in basements and fraternity houses. More recently, there are theaters that show these X, XX, XXX-rated films. It is hard to see many saving social graces for these films "but it paid the rent."

During the filming of a number of these pictures, Carla had an opportunity to meet a number of people associated with the filming. These were people who offered to help her out financially if she could perform sometimes outside of the range of the cameras. There were a number of men, usually somewhat older than herself, like sixty or seventy, who would pay her two or three hundred dollars to "do her act." And it was an act. Carla really never got turned on sexually with any of these "dates," and eventually gave up the movie making altogether for this more lucrative field. She was not getting anywhere with her movie career anyway, and she still hoped "to meet the right guy," although by now she was in her thirties and time was moving on. Her daughter was almost grown up, and had actually gone back to Michigan to live with the grandparents. Carla was alone. She decided not to marry for convenience anymore, and was still hoping to find the right man, but things were getting a little more difficult. She still hoped maybe to get a big part in "a real movie" and a chance to show that she still had "some class." But the parts were few and far between. She decided not to make any more X-rated films, because they had "used me too," and decided from thereafter, she was going to be the one to use others.

One day she got a call from a lady who had referred a number of "dates" to her in the past. This lady asked her if she could possibly do her a very big favor.

There was an older man who had been very important to this lady and had thrown an awful lot of business her way and a lot of cash as well. He had a favorite girl whom he dated, but she was out of town, and it was not clear when she would come back. He was looking for another playmate, and the lady wanted to know if Carla would help out. She did advise Carla that he liked "rough stuff." Rough stuff, in the vernacular of the streets, means somebody who enjoys sado- masochistic sex play. Frequently what this means is that the man enjoys making believe that he is beating up, whipping, tying and gagging, or even stabbing and mutilating the girl. Ladies who are experienced at this kind of activity can make a very large income. It is a dangerous business, though, because sometimes the actors get carried away. The man sometimes really does intend to play out the part, but makes mistakes. That is why it's called "rough stuff." Carla said she didn't want to have anything to do with it and never had done that kind of thing before. She wasn't about to start. She had been used too much in her life, and was not going to be used by anybody for anything like that. The lady pointed out, however, that Carla had owed her quite a bit of money.

It seems that on several occasions she had referred people to Carla for "dates" and never got her commission. The amount was something over four or five hundred dollars, she wasn't sure. She told Carla that she had been considering asking some friends to come over and collect the money, but had held off until this time. Now, she was going to give Carla a chance to have the debt forgiven. All Carla would have to do was take this "date," do her a favor and she would forgive all the rest. The man had already taken care of her commission, and she had assured him that Carla would like to meet him. She insisted that this man was not a nasty person and not really rough. He just liked to play and enjoyed games. Besides, he was a cripple. He could hardly use his legs, and spent most of his time in a wheelchair. How much could he really hurt her?

Carla agreed to do it. It was probably the most fateful decision of her life.

Her date's name was Charles. Later on, she called him Chuckles. He was a big man, over six feet tall, and weighed about two hundred and thirty to two hundred and forty pounds, but he spent most of his time in a wheelchair. He had trouble getting up and sitting down because of a bad back. He was not actually paralyzed, but it was difficult for him to get around easily, and he explained that to Carla. Because of his problem, his sexual activity was limited, and his wife just didn't understand how to please him. He had been having fun with one of Carla's friends for a long time, and he thought he would like to try it with somebody else.

Besides, his other friend was away. "He only wanted to play games," she recalled. The games were really not very demanding at first.

Carla was supposed to take off all of her clothes and act like a bad little girl for being naked. She would have to allow him to spank her for being naughty. She would have to say to him, "Please don't spank me, daddy." Or, "I've been a bad little girl, I know, daddy. Please be nice to me." Or, "I won't do it anymore, I promise. I'll be a good girl. Can I give daddy a kiss to make up?"

Later, there were other variations of the game, but they were all make- believe, and they were really "like making a movie." Carla thought she would enjoy this part, and it was really a lot easier than making a film.

She got to like Chuckles, and he got to like her, a lot. Chuckles was a wealthy man, and he had lots of "class." If you mean by "class" a Mercedes Benz, a house in Beverly Hills, a beach house in Malibu and an airplane, he had lots of "class." He also had a wife and some grown children, and he was sixty-five years old.

He set Carla up in an apartment in Beverly Hills. It was the nicest place she had ever lived in. She bought white rugs and white furniture. There were black accessories, and everything was leather and fur and glass and chrome. It was just like a movie from the thirties. She finally had "class" and lots of it. She knew this was what she had always dreamed of, and she-knew that it had to go on so that she wouldn't wind up scrubbing floors like her mother. She had to convince Chuckles to make it permanent. She had to get him to divorce his wife and marry her instead. It would be her fifth and last marriage, and she had to think it through carefully.

Chuckles was reluctant to get a divorce because it would mean, in California, that he would have to give half of his wealth to his wife.

There is a community property law in California. This means that everything that is accumulated by a couple during the course of their married life is divided by two should they divorce. Since Chuckles had been married to his wife for forty years, almost all of his wealth was accumulated during that time and belonged in equal part to his wife. Carla had to convince him to give up that half so that he could live with her "and make it legal." She did not want to just be a "kept woman," and she did not want to "hide in a corner." She tried everything she knew. She "gave him what he wanted." He liked that, but he was still not sure. She finally had to threaten to leave him and break up with him. This was really more than Chuckles could handle, and finally he agreed to get the divorce. It cost him an awful lot, but he went through with it.

Eventually, he was too uncomfortable staying in Beverly Hills where-his ex-wife and his children still lived. Chuckles and Carla decided to move to Palm Springs. The whole idea really appealed to Carla. Afterall, Palm Springs was the place where all the movie stars and millionaires congregated, and they had a lot of class in Palm Springs. They looked at several places, and finally decided to buy something on a golf course condominium development.

A golf course condominium is a concept which probably began in Palm Springs. What it means is that a developer gets a very large piece of property in the desert. He takes the raw desert and converts it into a "Garden of Eden." A virtual paradise is made overnight. Giant holes are dug in the desert and coated with plastic and asphalt, and then filled with water to create lakes. Whole tracts of land are sprinkled and grass planted so that the entire desert turns into a carpet of green. Fully grown palm trees are brought in by the dozens and scores of dozens to create an oasis in the desert. There are lakes and waterfalls, streams and little bridges. There are golf courses and fairways and greens, and tennis courts, and a pool for every house. There, of course, is a clubhouse with a ballroom and a bar, and a locker room. All of this springs up virtually overnight.

These places are not cheap, and the least expensive can be had for one hundred fifty thousand dollars. The most expensive go well over a million per house. One of the concept's main selling points is that you can have a house on the fairway of a golf course. You can sit in your backyard and watch the rolling green of the fairway or the golfers approaching the putting green. Or maybe you can just relax beside your pool and look at the snow-covered mountains in the middle of February with the temperature at the poolside of eighty-five. As George S. Kauffman once said, "It's what God would do if he had the money."

It was to one of these places that Carla and Chuckles moved. It was everything that Carla had ever dreamed about. She was finally living the life that she was meant to live. There was golf, and tennis, and she began to learn both. There was the country club dining room where she could dress up in her black sequin gowns and her white silks. Her silver lame sheathes and her white mink stole all fit in beautifully. There were parties for everything. There were Christmas parties and July fourth parties. There were Valentine parties and New Year's parties. There were Halloween parties, and there was even a Bastille Day party. Most of the parties consisted of "drinking and fun." Most of the people who attended the parties thought the drinking was the fun, and they enjoyed themselves immensely. Carla met some "classy people." She met people there who never knew what it was to work a day in their lives. Most of the women had never touched a broom or a scrubbing brush in anger or in earnestness.

Her fears of winding up her life like her mother, working as an old lady on her knees, evaporated as did the Chanel No. 5 perfume on her elbows on a warm day in Palm Springs. It was like a fairytale come true. She was Snow White, and Chuckles was her Prince Charming.

But like so many fairytales, there is always a catch. Chuckles really was not Prince Charming. He never was. Carla just wanted him so desperately to be like that that she made believe for a long time. Chuckles really was interested in Carla, because she made his fantasies come true. He became more and more insistent that they play their "games" daily. He wanted to have her pose in all kinds of unusual positions. He began taking Polaroid pictures of her in these positions, and finally she had to limit him "to one roll of film a day." Their sexual life became more and more restricted, as Chuckles preferred to get his sexual pleasures from watching Carla in almost a voyeuristic way, as she posed for him in unusual states of dress and undress. Sometimes he would like to have her bending over as though she was about to be spanked. 'On other occasions, he wanted to see her skin reddened after the spankings, and would have to do that first in order to take a good picture. There were occasions when he wanted her to pose in athletic stances for long periods of time while he took the picture, and made her most uncomfortable. There were other scenes of bondage in which she would have to be tied to bedposts or to ladders, or saw horses. He finally had to install a gym in the house instead of the playroom for their own "special kind of play." Chuckles' games were beginning to interfere with the tennis and the golf. Carla was becoming more and more compromised and more and more "used." It became harder and harder for Chuckles to get aroused, and he had to go further and further in the games.

Eventually, according to Carla, Chuckles wanted to see "more and more blood." He would create games in which Carla would have to act as though she had been stabbed. They had a knife which they would place between her left arm and her chest, smear it with blood and then Chuckles would take a picture as though she had just been stabbed. Of course, instead of blood, they used catsup and red ink, although Carla said she began thinking maybe he wasn't going to be satisfied with that either.

The games got more serious and the paddling got harder. On one occasion, Chuckles hit her really hard with the paddle, and she thought she had hurt herself and had maybe broken a bone. She was bruised for several days, and started to worry about how far he was going to go. He promised to take it easy, but he seemed to lose control too often.

One night, it was Halloween and they had just come back from a party in which Chuckles had dressed up like Dracula, and Carla, appropriately enough, like Elvira (the lady on the L. A. television channel who shows horror movies).

Chuckles thought it would be fun to play "the game" that night, as he did almost every night. Carla told him she was too tired. But Chuckles pointed out that he hadn't gotten his roll of pictures taken that day, and that was their deal. He wanted to hold her to the deal.

She wanted him to continue to provide the money which allowed her to go to the parties and tennis matches which she had come to feel were so important in her life. She agreed to play the game once again.

"He probably was turned on by the party," she later recalled. Eventually what happened was that he seemed to lose control. She recalls that he tried to paddle her "real hard" with the paddle, and he "hit me a little too hard." She grabbed the paddle away from him, and almost pulled him out of his wheelchair. "I guess he got scared and got angry too. He picked up the knife that we used for a prop, and swung it at me for real." Apparently, he cut her on the thigh, and she started to bleed. She thought he was going to start again and try to stab her for real. She doesn't know exactly what happened after that because she struggled with him for the knife. She remembers wresting it from his hand and his falling out of the chair, and she remembers her getting ahold of the knife and starting to hit him with it, point first. She stabbed him over and over again. She does not remember how many times. He was such a big man that he kept struggling with her, she recalled, "until there was blood all over." She finally realized the struggle was over and the he was not moving. She thought he might be dead, and apparently, he was. It was then that she went into a panic.

Rather than call the police and tell them that the game had gone wrong, Carla lost control of her thinking and her senses. She took the knife and washed it off and then hid it in a drawer. She washed her entire body off and took a shower and cleaned the blood off of herself and her clothing. She then put on her nightgown and called the police. She told them when they arrived that there had been three or four intruders in the house. There were two or three men and one woman. They had come into the house and attacked Chuckles for reasons she couldn't understand. They had killed him. She had heard him just at the end calling out to her. She had come into the room. He was bleeding, and she might have gotten some of the blood on her, as she tried to cradle his head in her arms. She did not really get a good look at the intruders, but she thought they were Mexicans or Latins of some kind. They had bushy hair and dark complexions. They were running past her in the darkened hallway. It was hard to see. It was late at night, and she was not sure. She was half asleep. She knew there was a woman and two or three men.

Most of the golf course condominiums are surrounded by high walls and have guarded gates. The gates are manned by private security police dressed like state troopers or city policemen, and most of them are armed. They have lists of the visitors who are coming in to visit the residents of the condominiums. In addition, they check on tradespeople, take the license numbers of entering cars, and look for strangers. There were no strangers that entered the condominium that evening or even that afternoon that could not be accounted for. There were not two or three Mexicans and a woman, nor any combination remotely similar to that. The police became highly suspicious of Carla's whole story, but tried to check it out.

They wound up checking on Carla's background and interviewing a number of her former friends. They even interviewed the lady who had introduced her to Chuckles. They found out about some of Chuckles' unusual interests, and thought that might have something to do with his death. They interviewed Chuckles' ex-wife, who told them what she knew about Carla. She even said that she did not think Carla was the one who was responsible for the murder, but probably some of her unsavory friends should be investigated. They even interviewed Chuckles' children. One of his daughters recalled that she knew, Carla briefly and thought that she "didn't have the brains of a cucumber." She pointed out that indeed if Carla had killed Chuckles, it was a foolish mistake, because in doing so, Chuckles' estate went to his children. Chuckles and Carla had signed a pre-nuptual agreement which indicated that if he died before five years of the marriage had elapsed, his estate would go to his children. All that Carla would get would be the house in Palm Springs. Killing him would be a rather foolish move to make since they had been married for only a year and a half. Maybe she did have the brains of a cucumber, but the police thought it might be worthwhile looking into this matter further. Carla's motivation did not seem to be sufficient, at least at this early stage. There was not any great amount of insurance available either. They continued the investigation.

Carla came to like one of the detectives on the case. His name was Howard, and he reminded her of William Powell in some of his early movies. He was smooth and suave and had a nice little moustache just like William Powell. She felt she could trust him. He seemed to like her too. He seemed sympathetic and understanding, and believed her story, she thought. She told him that she was deathly afraid that the Mexicans would come back and get her. She added that she thought she saw them hovering and hanging around the house in the dead of the night. She wondered if she could get some protection against them. He tried to reassure her as much as possible, and finally suggested that maybe she ought to go back to Michigan and visit her family for a few weeks until the investigation could proceed further and they could find the culprits. She followed his advice, and did indeed return to Michigan, and stayed with her family, and had a reunion with her daughter.

When she came back a few months later, the investigation had proceeded no further, and Carla was left alone in the big house at the golf course. She did not have much money, because the estate was going to go to Chuckles' kids.

There was some cash in the bank, but she was beginning to wonder how she could handle things. She didn't want to sell the condominium, and now that she was a Widow she had no source of income. She certainly could not go back to her earlier line of work. She had too much "class" for that. Probably the only thing to do now was to find husband number six, a thing she thought she would never have to do. Even though she was forty, she still retained her good looks, and she still looked like "Snow White," especially to a number of the widowed and divorced men who played golf at the country club.

"Buzz" was one of these. He was a retired investment banker who had been widowed some years earlier. He had no family and was, as he told her, a lonely man. He felt terribly sorry for Carla in her widowhood, and wanted to help and protect her. She told him that she was afraid all the time that the Mexicans would come back and hurt her, so "Buzz" offered to help as much as he could. He even offered to move in and keep her company, sleeping in another bedroom, just to keep her safe. He knew in his heart that she had never done anything to hurt Chuckles. Even though one of the detectives assigned to the case by the district attorney spoke to him when he announced his plans to marry Carla, he felt that they were simply persecuting her and harassing her. They got married a few months later, and the murder investigation went on.

The detectives kept coming around and asking questions and talking to Carla. They kept suggesting that there was no evidence of any Mexicans or anybody else coming into her house that night. They pointed out that she seems to have been the only one who had seen them.

There ensued a number of calls to the local police department from Carla indicating that she had been harassed, attacked and even raped by three Mexican men and one Mexican woman (who watched) on several occasions. Each time her husband was out of the house, and each time no one saw the intruders. Each case was investigated, and no arrests were made. Carla began to believe that no one believed her and, in retrospect, she began to lose her grip on reality. It became difficult for her to know which was real and which wasn't real, whether she was attacked and brutalized or whether she imagined she was. She didn't know whether Chuckles was killed by three intruders, or whether she had done it herself. She was no longer sure whether her new husband, "Buzz," really loved her or was just using her like everyone else did, for sex.

Finally, on Halloween, she invited "Buzz" to go out into the desert with her in some secluded spot, so they could make love. Their sex life had not been going very well of late, and "Buzz" eagerly accepted the invitation. They drove out to a secluded and isolated spot that he knew about. They spread a blanket on the sand under the Halloween moon. They made love like they had never done before, and "Buzz" was filled with warmth and love. Carla suggested that he lay on his belly and relax and she would rub his back, and maybe they could do it again if he had the energy.

As "Buzz" lay there, he suddenly felt a sharp pain in the back of his head and this whirring sound, and then again. He turned and saw Carla, for the third time smashing at him with a hammer. He tried to grab her hand, and she struck him a glancing blow the third time. She seemed to be out of control and confused. She said she didn't know what she was doing. She told him that nobody believed her. Nobody wanted to believe her, and that if he were found battered and beaten by the police out in the desert, someone would finally believe that "they" were trying to get her. Even "Buzz" had too much, and left. He finally went to a lawyer, and was advised to report the matter to the district attorney.

Carla was confused and agitated. She went home and swallowed a bunch of pills. Later, she called the hospital and said she had made a suicide attempt, and was admitted.

It was while in the hospital that the sheriff's deputies came and arrested her.

Later, at the trial, the district attorney told the jury that Carla had made up the whole story. He felt that there never was any love play that had gone bad. He pointed out that Carla had tried to hide the evidence of the murder, and made up the story of the intruders by her own admission. He told the jury that Carla had planned the whole thing in advance. She had premeditated the murder of Chuckles, and had killed him because she couldn't wait for the five years of their pre-nuptual agreement to expire. She just would kill him now, get the house, and find somebody else. He pointed out that she did find somebody else, and tried to kill him too. He proposed to the jury that all the stories she gave about being mixed up and having the sado-masochistic love play go out of control, and not knowing when things were real and unreal were products of her own imagination. He said that the psychiatrists and psychologists that had been brought in by the defense attorneys had all been taken in by Carla because she was such a good actress. This was a fact that had never been proven on any stage or screen before, but the district attorney was able to get the jury to believe it.

They found Carla guilty of murder in the first degree, and the judge sentenced her to twenty-five years to life in state penitentiary.

Whether Carla really did lose contact with reality and couldn't tell when the sex game became a death game is not clear. The fact is that she never really did have a good hold on reality throughout her entire life. She had always felt that she was being used, and had always tried to use others. The latter had never really worked, and while it appeared that other people had used her, nobody had come out a winner.

She finally had had a taste of "class," as she saw it. In addition, she had played the biggest role in her life. She made television and the newspapers, and even some magazines. She even may have been able to pull off an off-beat movie, called…

A NEW WORD FOR MURDER

CHAPTER 10

"God Made Me Do It"

In some people the ability to be reasonable and to think logically is distorted from the outset. Emotional feelings are accepted as logical feelings. Magic replaces reason, and the magic can be of the black variety. Tracing the core of the problem and understanding the mind of the murderer, in some cases, is easy to do. Trying to know how to change it is the real puzzle.

Hector Arturo Lopez was, unlike his namesake, neither born son to the King of Troy, nor destined to be a prince and hero of the Grecian wars. He was actually born in a farm community some thirty miles west of San Salvador, the capitol city of the republic of El Salvador. His family left there when "the troubles" began. That was sometime in the early 1980's. They moved to California to earn a living and to make their lives more full and complete. Hector grew up working as a hand in the fields near his home, along with his father. They actually worked for a large corporation in San Salvador.

The corporation was owned by people they never saw, but they made enough money to provide food and clothing for the family, and felt that they lived a good life. Hector only went to a few grades of elementary school. He learned to read and write before the family finances dictated that he would leave school when he was twelve. By the time he was sixteen, he had grown to almost his full size. Hector was strong and healthy and hardened by the ten to twelve hours he worked out in the fresh air and sunshine every day.

He spent much of his time, when not working, in reading religious pamphlets and books. These were provided by the priest at Our Lady of Guadalupe, the local church. Because he was the only one able to do so, he would read them to his three younger sisters. He felt that it was important to help them in their religious education as well. He was always seen as being "a good boy" throughout the community.

He went to church with his mother and sisters regularly, not only on Sundays, but on special feast days and special Saints days, and he was a devout believer. His father was not especially religious, but did join with the mother in hoping that Hector might be noticed by the local priest, Father Antonio, and, therefore, sent to the city for further religious education at no cost to them. But this never came about, so Hector continued to work the fields and help the family. Hector later recalled that his father always had mixed feelings about his being religious and devout. He thinks he heard his father mumble on one or two occasions to his mother that "They'll make him a queer." He felt that Hector was better off working in the fields anyway. It would be best to give up his interest and preoccupation with religion and God, and turn that over to the priests and the nuns.

Finally, when the troubles began with the rebels or Communists, depending upon your point of view, it became clear that there was going to be a lot of turmoil in the country. Many people would either be put out of work or even forced into taking sides. Young men were being drafted on both sides to be soldiers. Villagers were forced to take sides one way or the other. Hector's father wrote to a relative in the United States. He though it was time to leave the country, and in fact some money was sent from the relatives for the mother, father, and Hector to leave for California. The plan was to take a plane from San Salvador to Los Angeles, get a job in the city and later when some money was accumulated, to send for the three younger sisters. They were left with Mr. Lopez' sister in a nearby town, and the promise was that they would be coming to join the rest of the family shortly. Hector remembered feeling sad at leaving his sisters with his aunt, but he felt that this was probably the best decision and that God was watching over them, and no harm would come to them.

Hector recalled that when he got to the plane in the city of San Salvador, while at the airport, he began to hear "the voice" again. He feared that he had been shut off from the voice for a while, and hadn't heard it for some time. He thought that the voice was that of "The Holy One." It had been communicating with him for some time, probably since he was thirteen or fourteen years old. He knew that the voice was holy and righteous because it told him important things. It told him how to live his life and how to remain pure and wholesome. It told him what to stay away from and what evil forces there were around. This time, the voice told him good things, especially good about his trip. It talked about going to America and about leaving the Communists to go to the new country where things would be better and cleaner.

This was not always the case with the voice, though. Sometimes it used to tell him that it was unhappy with him and that he was bad. He felt its purpose was only to lead him into righteous paths and to avoid sin and to avoid profaning his body. He remembered that the voice had been especially serious about profaning his body when he was first ready to hear it.

When he was thirteen, Hector began hearing some kind of thoughts or sounds or ideas, he wasn't sure. He later knew that it was the voice and that it was helping him. He said that he always knew that he was different from other boys. He felt different inside of himself, and he knew that he was not like the others. The voice said that this was true. It said that he had been picked out by God for holy work. He felt blessed by this revelation, and tried to do whatever the voice told him to do. The voice told him that touching himself in his private parts was an abomination. It pointed out that the devil probably was the agent who caused him to do this when he was thirteen. The warm feelings that he had in his groin were clearly the work of the Evil one.

Satan caused these feeling to seem good, and maliciously caused Hector to think that they were good. This was done in order to capture his immortal soul.

The voice told him how important it was to reject these evil feelings and the thoughts that came with them. He had fought them ever since. He knew that other boys and young men did not fight against them, and they probably were doomed to eternal pain and the damnation of hell. He felt sorry for them, and realized that the devil probably had sent demons and witches in the forms of young girls and young women to tempt him and the other boys. He knew that it was his mission in life to reject those temptations and to warn others as well.

Unfortunately, most of the others fell to the temptation and even began acting out their abominable wishes.

The fallen ones began to abuse themselves sexually. Later, many of them began to involve themselves with the witches and demons in the form of girls at the cost of their very souls. Hector always knew that this was evil and that he must avoid it. He remained pure. He felt that he was a pure as the white robe worn by the blessed mother on the statue in the great cathedral in San Salvador. He had seen that once when he was younger, and had never forgotten it. He vowed that he would remain true to her for the rest of his life.

When the family arrived in Los Angeles, Hector's father's cousin, who had originally sent the funds for the airplane fare, told them that he knew there would be work for them in the Coachella Valley. This is the area of Southern California east of Los Angeles, in which besides the desert resort communities of Palm Springs, Palm Desert, Rancho Mirage and others, there are lush, fertile fields where table grapes grow. There are also grapefruit and all varieties of citrus fruit, as well as dates to be picked. It is probably one of the richest agricultural areas in the country. The valley provides much work for individual laborers picking grapes and grapefruit, planting crops, and processing the various produce from the fields.

Hector's father got a job in the fields picking grapes and fruit. His mother was able to find a job working in the date packing plants in Indio, California.

Hector was able, because he was young and vigorous and good looking, to get a job as a busboy in one of the restaurants in the Palm Springs area. He remembered getting the job in a restaurant where the rich people went to eat their food. He recalled that a rich person would spend as much money for a meal for just himself as Hector made working in the restaurant for two weeks. He thought that maybe everybody who lived in this country for some time because rich, and this was good. Things within the family were good too.

With all three of the Lopez' working, the father, the mother and Hector, they were able to make more money in a week than his father had made in six months at home. Things, of course, were expensive, including rent and food and even clothing. But they were able to save their money, and within six months were able to send for the three girls. Hector was pleased that this came about and that the girls would be around so he could watch and make sure that they were protected against the evil forces which he knew existed everywhere.

Hector became even more aware of the evilness and satanic possession of others in his new job. The young men in the restaurant, even though they were mostly Mexicans and Hispanics life himself, seemed to be all possessed by the demons. They could only think about sex and lust. They talked constantly with each other about these matters. They embarrassed Hector when they would tease him about his own purity. He began to feel that they were making fun of him and, because of that, making fun of God. He knew that they, too, would be damned forever, just as the ones he met at home had been. He prayed for them as often as he could.

Hector went to church regularly, and he prayed for others, as well as for his own soul. There was much temptation in America. Every time you turned on the television, there was evidence of the work of Satan. There were pictures on the television that aroused the evil instincts which he had experienced in the past.

Sometimes he feared that he would be overcome by them. He saw pictures in newspapers and magazines, and the other busboys and waiters would sometimes tease him with them. They would show him dirty things which he knew were fiendish. They surely were inspired by the Evil One.

He had to fight hard to overcome these problems. Satan was strong.

Sometimes when Hector was sexually aroused, he knew that he was feeling the force of evil.

By the time he was nineteen he had reached his full size. He was five feet, ten inches, the tallest in his family. He weighed one hundred and eighty pounds, and it was all muscle and sinew. He would go out every day before work and run up and down the roads near his home in Indio. He got stronger and more energetic each time. He knew that doing this would help to drive out the demons. He knew that running five miles would tire him, but running ten would sometimes push away the evil thoughts. Sometimes when he ran even more, up to fifteen miles, he would start to get exhilarating thoughts and feel that he was finally reaching the purity and holiness that he had sought for his whole life.

It happened when he had been in the United States for about a year. He was learning to speak the language fairly well and succeeding in his job at the restaurant. The devil finally presented him with his greatest temptation. It would be the final test as to the fate of his soul for all eternity.

Hector knew that someday he must choose to marry and have a family, since he was not suitable for the priesthood. The idea of this was frightening to him, because he knew that it would involve his exercising sexual powers for a good purpose. He also knew that it would be very hard to avoid the evil thoughts which would overcome hi if he didn't deal with them correctly. He understood that he would have to choose a wife from among the most pious and pure girls in the community. This was hard to do because he was surrounded by so many of the other kinds. There were so many evil ones. He realized that he was becoming more and more attracted to the others.

There was a waitress at the restaurant where he worked who was older than he. She must have been as old as twenty-five. She tempted him sorely. She had a full body and large bosoms and warm, brown skin, and dark, shining, lustrous hair. She moved her body in a sensual way to entice him. She seemed to undulate whenever she moved. It was as though she knew it was tempting to him and caused evil thoughts and arousal in him. He was forced to fight this temptation every night that he worked. He thought that it probably would be better for him to leave this job and get away from this temptress of his soul.

He had talked to his father about leaving the restaurant, and wondered if he might get a job with the grapes. His father had advised him that he was really doing far better in the restaurant, and that he could move ahead in that business, someday becoming a waiter or even a head waiter. He could become eventually free of manual labor. Working in the fields would have no end point except for old age and infirmity. His father advised him to stay with the restaurant and to deal with the sexual urges "like any other man." Sometimes he felt that his father was an agent of Satan too, but he dismissed this thought as something put into his mind to confuse him.

The girl's name was Yolanda. She liked to brush by Hector sometimes in the restaurant, only to tempt and tease him. She would smile at him sometimes and even giggle and laugh when he would speak to her. She would ask him from time to time if he would like to take a walk with her. She told him how handsome he was and how strong he looked. She once said that his dark, curly hair was more attractive than her own. One time, she told him that his eyelashes were longer and more attractive than hers, and how did he manage to get this done? He knew that Yolanda was teasing and tempting and that she would only try to lure him into eternal damnation. But he found himself being pulled further and further into her web.

The voices which he had heard were becoming dimmer. He had the feeling that he was losing touch with the Holy One and that God was abandoning him because of his obsession and interest in Yolanda. He thought that he was finally reaching the ultimate struggle for his soul. And he was terrified lest he lose.

He began having episodes of cramps and pains in his stomach. The pains were severe, and he had to stay home from work on more than one occasion. When he stayed home from work, the cramps got better and did not seem to bother him until he was ready to go back the next day. His father told him to ignore the cramps and pains and to return to work, or he would lose his job. His father pointed out that there were many others who would like to have a job as good as his. Whatever reason he had for "playing sick" was not good enough to jeopardize his career and his future.

"There are many of your friends who are now dying back in the fields at home," his father pointed out. "They were drafted by the Reds, and others were drafted by the government. It doesn't really matter. They're all dead now or about to die. You have it good here. You have a good job and a place to stay in a free country. Don't throw it all away with a bellyache. Be a man. Go back and act like a man."

Hector knew that in some way his father was encouraging him not only to go back to work, but to deal more directly with Yolanda. He felt this urge from inside of him, and he resolved that he would have to come to grips with this problem once and for all.

Possibly, if he could deal with this problem, he would be able to hear the voice of the Holy One again. Possibly, if he confronted Yolanda once more and wrestled with Satan, he would win out and then he would be worthy of God and God's attention. He decided to make the effort.

Hector went back to work and, of course, Yolanda seemed concerned about him. She came over and held him by the shoulders, one hand on each of his shoulders, gently kneading the muscles. She said, "Are you better now, my little virgin?" She smiled and pressed her belly toward him. "Do you think you're going to be able to stay here for a few days just so I can look at your beautiful body?"

Hector forced a smile and said, "I will be all right now, Yolanda. I am sure that I will be healthy again."

"How healthy do you think you are, Hector? Do you think you're healthy enough to wrestle with me?"

Hector knew then that this was a challenge from Satan. He knew that Yolanda wasn't speaking directly to him but that the evil one was talking. He knew, too, that Yolanda was not simply inviting him to some sexual encounter, but that Satan was giving him the ultimate temptation to wrestle for his soul. He also knew what he had to say and do.

"I think I could wrestle with you, Yolanda. I think I'm ready to do that."

"Don't be so sure of victory, my saintly friend. I'd love to be the first one to bust your cherry. Why don't you come over to my apartment this evening, after your shift. We'll have a glass of wine, and we can talk about wrestling."

All through that night, Hector was filled with agitation. His stomach was cramping as it had never cramped before. His skin was creeping with perspiration and, at the same time, he felt cold and gooseflesh all over it. At the same time, he began to feel the warm stirrings in his groin and a swelling which he could not control. He knew that the power of Satan was overwhelming and that he would have to cope with it once and for all.

When everything was cleaned up after work, Yolanda was in fact waiting for him. She said, "Let's go over in my car. I can take you home later if you want, or maybe you'd like to stay the whole night with me." She smiled in a knowing way and winked her eye at him. She told him that she had some wine in her apartment, and they would have a few drinks together to relax and calm down, because she, too, was excited at the prospects of being with him.

They arrived in a few minutes at her nearby apartment in one of the low- rent areas near the hotel district, and she poured him a large glass of red wine. She had some herself, and while drinking, began to loosen her clothing. As she did this, she turned on her phonograph to the music of some tango rhythms. He knew that now he had reached the ultimate test and challenge for his immortal soul. He began to feel that he was failing. He could not hear the voice of the Holy One to help him. He was not able to summon the courage to resist his carnal lust. His sexual drive was overwhelming, and he thought that he would be lost. But he could not help himself. Yolanda embraced him and gradually removed his clothing as well as her own. It was warm in her apartment, and perspiration on their bodies began to emerge. Eventually, they were engaged in sex play, and shortly that led to sexual intercourse. Hector had never known anything like this before. Even when he had touched himself in the past, he had never been so aroused and so excited. He felt that his soul had been lost forever, and the strange thing about it was he didn't seem to care. Yolanda was smiling and laughing, and the two of them were carried away with their passion.

When they were finished and he felt the gradual ebbing of his exhilaration and lust, feelings of guilt, remorse and violation rose within him. He realized that he had finally lost his soul and that it might be gone forever. He realized he had given into the very evil that he had feared all of his life.

He began to pray as he had never prayed before to God. He feared that God would not listen. He thought that probably he was now the property of Satan. But with tremendous energy and overpowering force, he began praying to the Lord to forgive him and to show him a way to redeem himself.

Yolanda, in the meantime, was lying flat on her back with her eyes closed and a sort of half-smile on her face. Her arms were stretched out on the bed. She was not speaking, but sort of humming in a low tone to the music on the phonograph. As he looked at her and prayed, he realized that she actually showed the stigmata of the devil. He could see small protrusions in her forehead which he knew to be the horns of Satan. She had hidden them from his view during their lustful violation of his virginity. He began to see the evidence of the cloven hoofs of Satan on her feet underneath the covers. He knew that they were there and had only been disguised from him through some demonic spell. He knew, too, that there was a hidden forked tail. Probably she was not even a woman, but a demon.

He was betrayed, violated and defiled. He prayed to God for help. Finally, in God's mercy, He answered him: "Kill the demon, kill the demon, kill the demon." The voice was clear. It was insistent, and it was demanding. He knew that God had given him an order. The only way to save his soul and probably that of thousands of others was to destroy this Satanic messenger, this witch, this sorceress, this demon who had entrapped or tried to entrap his soul. If he could only kill her now, he would be saved.

He got up from the bed. She remained there, writhing and moving to the sounds of the phonograph. She said something, or mumbled something to him about a beer in the kitchen, and he did go to the kitchen. There he found a very large butcher knife which she used to slice bread. He knew that God had placed it there for his use and that his message from God was clear. His mission was preordained, probably from the beginning of time. It was his job to once and for all destroy Satan. He would be blessed among all men and loved above all by God for finally destroying the Evil One.

He grasped the knife as though it were a holy instrument. He kissed the blade and the handle and took it back with him to the bedroom. She still laid there with her eyes closed as though she did not realize what he was about to do.

He knew that Satan had tremendous powers and that Satan would create a tremendous struggle with him as soon as the Evil One knew what Hector was about to achieve, so he struck quickly and decisively. He plunged the blade with all of the strength of his one hundred and eighty pounds into Satan's chest. He aimed it as closely as he could to the heart of the fiend. The blood gushed forth and spread about him. Satan writhed and screamed, but it didn't last very long, because Hector began plunging the knife again and again into the form of the demon. Later, it appeared that he made twenty-seven separate thrusts into the body of the Evil One.

Eventually, Hector was covered with blood from Lucifer's body, and the bedroom was soaked with the same fluid that once gave life to the carrier of the demon. He sat at the side of the bed staring at the floor and smiling. The voice of God had been obeyed. God smiled upon him, and he was blessed.

The scream, which had been brief, apparently had been heard by someone in the next apartment. Within some minutes, he did not know how long, several policemen came. They saw Hector sitting at the side of the bed covered with blood, the knife still lying on the floor. They took Hector into custody and handcuffed him, and took him away to the prison. The never did understand what a wonderful thing he had achieved nor had great was his accomplishment. He had saved the world and probably saved all of them from the clutches of the devil and from eternal damnation and the fires of hell. They didn't treat him with the respect that he knew he deserved, but he also knew that God would reward him and remember him.

Later, when a psychiatrist came to visit him, he was able to tell the story in some detail, because the doctor was willing to listen. He suspected that the doctor didn't really believe everything, but that didn't matter, because Hector knew it was true. He still heard the voices of God and his angels from time to time reassuring him that he had done well. They told him that he was blessed above all, and that his time on earth was only a passage, leading eventually to paradise.

Hector's story and its ultimate outcome is seen by most medical people, certainly by all competent psychiatrists, as a rather typical example of a schizophrenic disorder. Paranoid notions which center around demonic possession are not unusual, especially focusing on religious themes in the Hispanic culture from which Hector came. In more secular societies, the paranoid notions which exist are centered around Communists, homosexuals, fascists, the FBI, CIA, the KGB and other organized groups. In religious cultures, it is frequently the devil and demons. Research into historic records indicates that this was the traditional view in medieval times toward the mentally ill. That is, that they are not sick, but possessed by Satan and his minions. Some groups today still think that is true.

Hector's voices, of course, were voices and sounds coming from his own mind which were misinterpreted as outside influences. His sexual continence and celibacy were really the products of his terror and the fear of intimacy and closeness to other people. Schizophrenics have great difficulty in relating in a meaningful way to others, and the sexual act sometimes can be frightening and overwhelming. Hector's sexual conceptions and notions were consistent with the diagnosis but, unfortunately, the diagnosis was never made, nor was he ever treated. People like this are able to be handled and treated if the disease is detected early. Certainly, a young boy who hears voices at the age of thirteen and fourteen, in most societies, would report them to his family. They would listen, and try to get help. Help would be available, and with medication and psychotherapy, a result such as this can be avoided. Unfortunately, in this case none of the above came to pass. As a result, the life of a young woman, who was possibly tempted herself by a good looking, energetic, handsome and bashful young man, was snuffed out probably before she ever realized it was even in danger.

There are not a few people who have said that God has driven them to acts of inhuman wickedness and destruction.

Of course, Hector's diagnosis of schizophrenia was confirmed by more than two expert witnesses. It was felt appropriate by the court to remand him to a state hospital for the criminally insane. The purpose of this is to place an individual with this kind of disease in a therapeutic facility where he can be treated for the illness until such time as he is deemed by the institution to be able to stand trial. Whether or not Hector will ever be adequately treated so that he can then return and stand trial for murder, which he committed under the delusion that he was doing God's work, is definitely questionable.

Ultimately, it may be that with the advances in medical science and our increasing understanding of the biochemistry and neurochemistry of the brain, this disease will be successfully treatable. Whether it will be too late for Hector is open to question. If, at some future date, he is in fact cured, it may well then be decided by a court that under the current law in California, the McNaughton rule will hold. That is, that a person who is laboring under the delusion that robs him of the ability to distinguish right from wrong is not guilty of the crime with which he is charged. This might be hard for the family of the young waitress who died so suddenly and violently to accept, but it is the law as it stands now. This is only a matter of speculation, as it may be many, many years before the question will ever have to be determined in his case.

In the meantime, Hector's quest for his road to salvation and paradise has resulted in the destruction of another young human life. His inability to distinguish reality from fantasy has caused the death of someone else. His confusion between sexual needs and demonic drives has caused the flowing of the life's blood of another person. Death has triumphed over life again. While death always is the winner in the tragedy of everyone's life, sometimes it comes far too soon. Sometimes the overwhelming need to exercise emotion and the instinctive drives deep within us can conquer the need for life in another person. When instinct reigns supreme, emotion controls, and reason disappears. Life becomes cheap, and a torrent of blood washes away the commandment, "Thou shalt not kill."

Thus, we have another situation, another death, and …

A NEW WORD FOR MURDER

CHAPTER 11

Bad Girls Die Young

By now it would seem that the sands of the desert are soaked with blood and have turned at least pink, if not brown, in color. Total strangers, business partners, friends, loved ones and relatives have all contributed to the flow of life emptied out into the desert in each of these cases. As we said before, killing someone that you love is usually the case, and killing someone close to you is a lot easier than finding a total stranger. This seems to be at the core of the problem.

Feelings run highest among those who are closest to each other. The inability to think clearly, to reason and to work things through to a logical conclusion seem to disappear among even the most logical among us.

Even those whom we have appointed to guard our safety and to protect us against evil doers can become the victims of this disease. Policeman are no exception. A man who has been sworn to carry out law and order and to protect the life and safety of the rest of us can be a victim as well.

"Can I give you my confession, Rabbi? I tried to find a priest or a minister, but I don't know where to look. I'm Jewish, but I knew that a priest isn't able to tell on me. Isn't a Rabbi under the same rules?"

"I killed my wife tonight. I think I killed her. I left her there in the apartment. She was unconscious, I think, but I think she's dead. She told me that she'd kill me. She said, "I'll kill you." We had this fight and I started to hit her. I think I choked her. She was unconscious. I don't know if she was dead. I just put something in her mouth, a gag, and I tied her hands a little bit. She was alive when I left her, but I think she's dead."

"I didn't know what to do. I wanted to go to L.A., and I went to L.A. to tell the paper about it. I wanted them to know that I didn't do it."

"I didn't know what to do. I wound up in Riverside. I was riding around in a fog. I was all mixed up. I wanted to see a priest or maybe a minister, but I couldn't find one. I finally came to Palm Springs. I came here to tell you. I don't know what to do? You can't tell on me, can you?"

Saul Levenson was a rather large man and still in apparently good physical condition for his sixty-eight years of life, but he was haggard and worn, and very tired. The Rabbi could see this. He appeared to be unshaven, and did look like he had been driving all night in a fog or in some other state of confusion. His story was frightening, and certainly not the usual kind of thing the Rabbi heard in his office.

Mr. Levenson had arrived early in the morning, just after morning Services, and came straight to the temple. He told the girl outside that he had to see the Rabbi, that it was a matter of great urgency and that it was a matter of life and death. Of course, the Rabbi made some time to see Mr. Levenson. He recognized immediately that it was a matter of unusual importance, and as the interview went on, he began to fear that it was even potentially dangerous. He was not sure what to do himself. This didn't usually come up in his congregation.

His congregation, like so many in sun belt communities, was made up largely of older people. They were retired couples in their sixties, seventies and even eighties. There was a large sprinkling, or even a deluge of widows and widowers. They came from Chicago and Seattle, from New York and Detroit. He even had some congregants from as far away as Toronto, Montreal and London. They came from wherever the sun didn't shine in the winter. They came to enjoy their declining years in the warmth of the desert and to protect their arthritic joints from the dampness of the northern and eastern climates. He sometimes thought of the town and especially his congregation as an elephants' graveyard, a place where the aging mammoths could come and congregate and lie down and die. Eulogies were one of Rabbi Margolis' strong points.

Rabbi Margolis really was not sure if Mr. Levenson was telling the truth, or if possibly he was deranged in some way. He did appear to be confused and agitated, and many of the things he said didn't quite make sense. Mr. Levenson would jump from topic to topic, and as he went on to tell his story, it became more and more evident to the Rabbi that he needed to get some outside help.

He decided he would try to calm this very disturbed man down a little bit and see if, in getting him to rest and relax, he could get a clearer picture of what was going on. He suggested that Mr. Levenson come with him to a small motel in town which was owned and run by an elderly couple who were members of his congregation. He took him over there himself, and introduced Mr. Levenson to the people. The Rabbi asked them if they could put him up in one of their rooms for a day or so until he felt more comfortable. They agreed, and showed Mr.

Levenson to one of their rooms. They gave him the key, and told him to try and get some sleep, since he looked very tired and run down. He thanked them, and locked himself inside of the room.

It was one of those small motels which, in Palm Springs, are called hotels.

There is a city ordinance which says there are no motels in Palm Springs and, therefore, every small place that has six or seven or eight bungalows or rooms is a hotel. This was one of them.

These are generally small, clean and neat places run by elderly couples. Usually, they have retired and invested their life's savings in a motel complex which they hope will make enough money to keep them financially secure, and also give them something productive to do that is not too strenuous. They usually are able to hire someone to clean out the place for them and they, in effect, run a "mom and pop" operation. Each of these small places has a little pool and jacuzzi, which they keep heated and which they use themselves, as well as for their guests.

These buildings originally were put up right after World War II when people first began to discover that it was only a short ride to Palm Springs from the city of Los Angeles. They would take their two-hour drive on a Friday afternoon or Friday evening and spend the weekend at "the Springs." It gave a lot of the middle-class people the feeling that they were living the same kind of life that the movie stars did. The movie stars, of course, had found Palm Springs, in the twenties and thirties, but the population explosion after World War II and the advent of better highways and, later, freeways made it open to everyone. A lot of small motels sprung up and did well in the forties and fifties. By the sixties, they began to get a little run-down, and by the seventies and eighties, they began to be used as "residential dwelling places." That meant that they could be rented by the month, by the season (that is, during the winter), or even by the year for ever diminishing rates. This was the kind of place that Saul Levenson came to for the final act of what he later called his "bad tragedy."

After the couple had left him alone in the room and he had carefully locked the door to make sure that no one could come in, he once again considered his predicament. He realized he had done something irretrievable. He could not bring back his wife. He knew that by now she was dead and the police must be looking for him. He realized that he had no place to go, and probably it was just as well if he were to die too. He found a table lamp with a long electric cord, and ripped it away' from the lamp. He felt that would be strong enough to strangle him if he hung himself from the light fixture in the ceiling. The cord was not long enough, and he had to look around for some string or some more cord to make it longer.

He tied the string together with the electric light cord, and then attached the end of the cord to the light fixture. He hung the loop from the fixture, stood on the bed and put it around his neck.

He felt that if he jumped off the bed, it would catch him in the act of falling and either break his neck or strangle him as he hung from the fixture. His calculations did not take into account that he was a relatively burly, five foot ten, one-hundred-and-ninety-pound man. By leaping from the bed in order to pull the cord tight, he also put tremendous strain on the cord and the fixture. Of course, as a result, when he did make his final leap, all he succeeded in doing was ripping the light fixture from the ceiling, resulting in a tremendous crash. As he lay on the floor, somewhat dazed from the fall, he decided that he couldn't waste any more time in his own self-destruction. He saw a gas heater in the corner of the room, turned it on full force and then placed his face against the grate in the heater. He hoped to die of suffocation and poison from the gas.

By this time, of course, the old couple had heard the crash and had decided that they had better call the police. They did so, and then fearing that something terrible had happened, went over and unlocked the door to the room with a pass key. When they came into the room, they were startled to see Mr. Levenson crouched in front of the gas heater trying to breathe in the fumes. The elderly man, who was about seventy-five, shouted, "Stop, don't do that, it's crazy. You must be crazy. What are you doing?" And his wife screamed at the same time.

Saul, by this time, was dazed and confused and angry. By his account, he didn't know for sure what was going on, except that the man was trying to stop him from doing what he had to do. As the man approached, Saul grabbed him by his shoulders and flung him aside. He swears that he didn't hit him, but it really didn't make much difference because as he flung him aside, the man's head went into the heater. It was made out of "some heavy metal or steel or something like that," according to Saul. Whatever it was made of, it was enough to crack the man's head open and to cause him to die. Saul did not realize he died at that moment, but he knew he had hurt someone else. Then he pushed the old lady aside too, and tried to leave the room and get away from all this destruction. As he left the entrance to the motel, the police arrived and ordered him to stop.

There was a struggle and he said, "There were three or four of them, I'm not sure if one of them or maybe two had a club. We mixed it up a while, and the next thing I knew they were hitting me on the head. I fell down, I guess. That's the last I remember clear. The next thing I knew they had me in jail."

Saul Levenson should have known something more about police procedure than he described. He had been a policeman in the city of Philadelphia for almost fifteen years before he was discharged. He reported that he had always been a good police officer and had enjoyed his work, and had hoped to make something of his life even though he had never finished high school. He said he only left school because "I had to go out and go to work to help my family."

Later, he finally was able to find employment and passed the test for the Philadelphia Police Department. He was "a good cop" and said, "I was up for promotion to Sergeant, but somehow they gave me a medical discharge instead of a promotion." He said he thinks that was because he injured himself and twisted his knee while he was working on duty, and that's why he got the discharge. He was unhappy about having to leave the police department, because he had seen such a great career coming for him with it. But he accepted his fate and adjusted.

He was able finally to find a job in Baltimore where he had some relatives, and became a bus driver. He worked as a bus driver for several years and then later, hoping to find a better life, moved to California where he worked again as a bus driver.

It was during this time that he and his wife divorced. They had been married for twenty years, but never had any children. He was never very happy with Sylvia. She was "a cold woman." They never really got along together in their marriage. They never had good sex. They never had children. And they never loved each other. He realized that his marriage wasn't going to get anywhere, and after twenty years he thought there was still time for him to make his life work again. He left his wife in Baltimore, and came to California for the sun and for the warmth and for a new life and a new beginning. He was strong and smart, and he found jobs without any trouble. He worked as a bus driver and then became a security man for one of the big California aviation companies. He even learned how to be a masseur, and he worked at that part-time as well.

Since he had divorced his wife, he was able to start getting around some more, and he started to go to Las Vegas. He began dating a lot of girls in Vegas, and sometimes they were prostitutes. He felt that that was probably the only way he was going to find somebody who was still young. Eventually, he wound up seeing one particular prostitute on a regular basis. She was thirty-one years his junior, but she seemed to like him. "She really liked me, and I could tell she was not really a bad girl. She just got into the wrong crowd. You know, she was born in Europe. She didn't know any better. Her family thought that her father was really an American. She was born right at the end of the war in France, probably her mother got knocked up by some G. I."

When they met, in 1976, she was thirty-one years old and he was sixty-two.

He had been separated from his wife for many years, and he was a lonely man, and she filled the void. He didn't care that she was a prostitute. He told himself that she wasn't really bad, and that he was going to help her to redeem herself. He knew she had a lot of troubles in her life, but he thought he could help her too. He had been around, and he knew about the world. He thought he could help her to reform and to "stop being a. bad girl." He would make her his wife and make her legitimate, and teach her how to be a masseuse. He would share his fortune with her and, indeed, he did have a fortune.

Ever since he got divorced, he had worked hard. He had had two jobs, sometimes even three, and lived very frugally. He had managed to save a lot of money, and he had won some gambling in Vegas too. By the time he got married, he had almost sixty thousand dollars in his bank account. He had told Marie, his thirty-one-year-old bride, that he was going to share it all with her and that they were going to live a happy life together. They might even have some children. This never came to pass, and through the six and a half years of their marriage, there was one problem after another.

Marie was, indeed, a troubled young lady. She had a number of physical problems. She was always sick, and she couldn't eat well. He thought that she was anorexic. He tried to take her to a doctor to get help, but she refused. He tried to feed her and to teach her physical culture, but she remained sick, and she didn't like to eat. She was thin, and sometimes he thought she was emaciated.

"No matter what I told her she wouldn't listen. She was headstrong, that one. Maybe it was her French background, I don't know, but she never would listen to me. I tried to tell her how to live good. I tried to tell her how to be good, but I guess underneath it all, she was still a bad girl." He began to be certain that even though he had found her a new profession and taught her how to be a masseuse, she was really at heart still a prostitute.

Together they started to earn a good income. They increased their savings until it was more than twice what he had when he first married her. He was planning finally to retire and maybe to move to Las Vegas, or maybe to Palm Springs and buy a little hotel. But she didn't want to do this.

She liked being a masseuse. She enjoyed taking care of important people, and she got a job at "one of the fancy clubs down near the beach." He knew that she was getting more and more involved in taking care of "millionaires and billionaires." He began to think that possibly she had some kind of sexual perversion, because she was always going over and taking care of some wealthy lady whom he described as "an influential person." He added, "She's such an influential person, I'm even afraid to mention her name." He began to be certain that this influential person was involved in a lesbian affair with his wife and plotting against him. He was certain that this woman, who was also married, was trying to cause his destruction. He wasn't sure why, except maybe she wanted to have Marie for herself.

During the year prior to the murder, he became more and more certain that this woman was out "to do me in."

As time went on, he became more and more confused. He began to think that this lady who was involved with his wife had "promised my wife a considerable amount of money after my death so I wouldn't charge her husband." He said he had done some masseur work for her husband, and that this man didn't want to pay his bill. When it was pointed out to him that it seemed somewhat inconsistent that a multimillionaire, much less a billionaire, would be concerned about the fees that a masseur was charging and try to avoid them by having him killed, he said, "I just don't know why. I don't understand these kind of people."

I had all kinds of papers. They took my money back from me." And he went on and on in a loose string of thoughts that didn't quite run together, and seemed to be filled with confusion and contradictions.

It became clear that Saul Levenson was increasingly confused over the past several years of his life. He had really not been able to understand what was going on around him. He even went to see a doctor in Beverly Hills at the insistence of his wife, but said this doctor

165

wasn't any help to him. He pointed out that his wife had asked him to take vitamin pills and other things to help him, but he thought that really "she was giving me hormones. She was putting me on steroids. I don't know what she was trying to do. I think she was trying to make my teeth harder."

Finally, in Saul Levenson's confusion and agitation, he began to realize that his wife, Marie, was truly plotting against him with her lesbian girlfriend. She had decided to get all of his money for herself, and was going to kill him. He accused her finally on that fatal evening of a plot to assassinate him. She told him it was silly and crazy.

She went on to tell him that he was crazy and he had been becoming crazier and crazier over the past few years. She knew that it was a terrible mistake to marry him, and she had to get rid of him. She knew she was a fool for ever thinking she could make it with an old man. She became more and more angry and hysterical, and spit flew from her mouth as she screamed at him. He saw her eyes widen with hate and rage, and he knew that if he didn't do something right away, she was going to kill him. So, he began to hit her. She hit him back, and tried to scratch him, and he hit her even harder. He began to choke her, then to squeeze her throat. Once she stopped moving and kicking, he wasn't sure whether he had killed her or not. He thought that possibly she was just knocked unconscious, and he thought he would make it look as though somebody had come in and robbed her. So, he stuffed a towel into her mouth and tied her hands behind her back with a lamp cord. He then got into his car and started driving away.

After he had gone for a few minutes, he thought possibly the towel he had stuffed in her mouth might have choked her, if she wasn't choked already. But it was probably too late. He would go to the newspapers and explain that he didn't mean to kill her and that it was all an accident. He then realized that that would not help him any because the newspapers would surely call the cops and turn him in. He then thought that maybe he needed to see a priest, to confess to a priest, because priests he knew could not reveal what was told in their confessionals.

Maybe a minister did the same thing, he wasn't sure. He wasn't Catholic, but he had heard about these things. He started driving around to churches at night but, of course, they were closed, and nobody was in.

He got back into his car and decided to go to Palm Springs where it was warm and where the sun would be out soon, and where he could think. When he got to Palm Springs and the sun had come up, he realized that going to a priest would not help him any. Maybe he should go to a Rabbi because, he was Jewish and had been raised that way, and maybe the Rabbi could understand him and tell him what he should do. He found the temple in Palm Springs, parked his car, went in, and asked to see the Rabbi.

He knew he should never have married a bad girl and that bad girls only cause grief to other people and to themselves.

After Saul Levenson had been arraigned and pleaded not guilty to the felonies of murder in the first degree against his wife and murder in the second degree against the hotel keeper and to assault with intent to kill against the hotel keeper's wife, who didn't die, he was sent for psychiatric evaluation.

It became clear during the initial phases of the psychiatric evaluation, and also later when he was examined by a psychologist, that he had what is known as an organic brain syndrome. He had many gaps in his thinking, and was unable to keep thoughts closely strung together or reasoned carefully. He was extremely irritable, and laughed sometimes at inappropriate times. Sometimes he began to cry very easily, especially when he was telling his tale of tragedy and woe. He was filled with regret and remorse, and extremely unhappy about all the terrible things he had done, and had been done to him.

He demonstrated a significant lack of recent memory. He couldn't remember names or dates or places. He got easily confused, and he thought the doctor who was examining him was a lawyer. He thought that his lawyer was actually a doctor, and got the two mixed up. He couldn't remember the name of his lawyer, and wasn't able to remember the names of any of the people he had met recently. His memory for the remote past was rather good, and this is typical of organic brain injuries. That is, he could remember his childhood, his elementary school, the names of teachers, friends he had as a kid, even his few years in high school. He remembered Philadelphia and eating places he went to, the friends he had on the police force, and adventures which he experienced there. He remembered several murders and crimes of violence in which he had been involved as a police officer, and described them in detail. He had much more difficulty in describing the events which had led him to be in jail, and even greater difficulty in talking about the simple things, such as what he had had for breakfast or what were the names of the other men he had met in prison.

It became clear that Saul Levenson had some kind of organic brain disorder and needed to be further evaluated. In fact, he was sent to a county hospital, to a prison ward for more testing. He was seen in the prison ward by a neurologist, who found that there were indeed abnormalities of his brain waves and unusual findings in his neurological exam. Saul probably had some softening of the brain and some history of small strokes over the past few years which had interfered with his thinking. A CT scan, that is, a computerized tomography study of the brain by x-rays, was done. It revealed that there were several areas of injury to his brain, some recent and some remote. Saul's brain was gradually dying, and in its death throes it began to affect the lives of those around him. His wife, of course, was the first victim, and the motel owner the second.

Saul never came to trial, because it was decided that he was incompetent to stand trial or to defend himself. This was because he was suffering from a disorder of his brain which robbed him of reason and the ability to comply with the requirements of the law. He is still, at this time, in a hospital where he was sent by the Court. He is gradually deteriorating, and when last seen he was unable to contain his bowel movements or control his urination all the time. He was having more and more difficulty speaking clearly, and it seemed to be only a matter of time before he would gradually have increased confusion and possibly total dementia. Most men who have dementia and softening of the brain do not commit murder. But then, most men are not ex-policemen who marry prostitutes thirty-one years their junior. Most men of sixty-eight are not physically able to pick somebody up and throw them across the room. Rarely, do they find themselves in physical combat with a woman more than thirty years their junior, who is filled with rage and hate and who verbalizes aloud all the things that they are afraid of hearing and who confirms all of their fears and suspicions.

Most people do not seek out Palm Springs as a place of refuge for erasing their crimes. This kind of behavior can go on anywhere, in your town or in the town or city nearby. It can, and it does. Probably right now some act of loss of control, of confusion and rage is happening. It can happen among those most close and dear to you, or even to you as well.

There are ways to deal with these problems. There are solutions. There are preventive measures. To any problem which people create, there is a solution which they can also devise. We should spend some time in exploring that, both for the good of our society and community, but also to protect our own lives and families. And thus, we finish another chapter on ...

A NEW WORD FOR MURDER

CHAPTER 12

Make My Day

Life is real and not a movie. it's not a story or a television drama. It's not a book, such as this One, or a comic strip. We spend so much of our time as we grow up with other media, though, that sometimes it's hard to draw the line.

Many of the people whom we have described have had great difficulty in drawing the line. It's up to us to help them and to help ourselves, if we hope to stay alive. The trail of the thin red line of blood lust and fear, here is where we have to begin to change things, to understand and to alter behavior before the fatal act occurs and the curtain falls.

When Clint Eastwood uttered the sure-to-become immortal words "Make my day" in one of his "Dirty Harry" films, he was about to shoot to death a vicious killer. In his role as "Dirty Harry" Callahan, an inspector of the San Francisco Police Department, Eastwood similarly executes numerous bad, very bad, and evil people. In doing so, he provides vicarious satisfaction for millions of people. The elimination of these detestable creatures from the screen by "Dirty Harry's" violent actions is applauded, and Clint Eastwood makes a fortune. This is the American way, and probably always will be. The problem is that in real life we cannot resolve issues by shooting the bad guys or eliminating people from the scene by dramatic means. People are rarely as evil and vicious as the villains in movies. Problems are rarely as black and white as they appear to be on the screen, even when the film is shot in technicolor.

Most of the issues which led to the killings in this book were the result of complex situations which had developed over a period of many years. Even the few instances of murder for profit in terms of robbery or the acquisition of dope and money were not as clear-cut as they might seemed had they been done in a film. People have complex characters and multiple motivations for everything that they do. Small things which might have changed in the stories of any of the people cited in this book could have resulted in an avoidance of the ultimate result, that is, the death of a victim or victims.

Even the multiple murder which occurred on the freeway might have been avoided if Charley Baxter had been more successfully treated as a youngster, or even a young adult, for his drug abuse problem. Since the use of amphetamines destroyed his ability to think, and finally created the delusions and hallucinations which resulted in the killings, it is probable that some earlier and more forceful intervention could have prevented the deaths of all those innocent people. It is less likely that this could have occurred in the case of Tom Winters, since it was not so much drugs as greed which wound up being the motivation for his activities. Even though drugs were involved in the genesis of the crime, the killing could have occurred over something else. This is the way that murders occurred in Prohibition times over alcohol, or killings still occur in "the mob" because of problems with gambling and skimming of profits or cheating "the wise guys." When greed is involved, successful intervention becomes a difficult problem to handle.

It is true, however, that in two of the other killings which we described in this book, the use of drugs was crucial, along with other factors. That is, in the case of Paul Gould, he allowed drugs to compound his problem of an organic brain syndrome. It is likely that if treatment had continued with him throughout his adolescence and early adult life, he never would have gotten into the situation which led to his crime. The same seems to be true in the case of the filling station killer, whom we have identified as Aubrey O'Neil. Both of these young men probably suffered from some kind of organic brain disorder. It showed itself early in life, and was either partially or inadequately treated or understood, both by the family and the physicians who had been consulted. The point being, that adequate treatment instituted early enough can, in fact, prevent worsening of the disorder and is an essential step in avoiding a tragic outcome.

This can be said for each of the other killings described in this book. A schizophrenic who kills because of a delusion about sex and evil women probably should have come to treatment years earlier. In modern psychiatry, the treatment of schizophrenia is probably as well documented as any other kind of medical therapy. The use of major tranquilizers, such as Thorazine, Mellaril, Stelazine, and many others is well known and widely used. These drugs probably have prevented huge amounts of violence in the past twenty to thirty years since their introduction. They have, in fact, been responsible for the tremendous decrease in the population at state hospitals all across the United States and in mental institutions around the world.

A psychiatrist is not in the position of Clint Eastwood playing a hero in a film. He has to wait a lot more than two hours for the happy ending to occur. He is not able to make quick decisions and effect rapid solutions to crimes with a .44 Magnum automatic. The thing that can "make the day" of a psychiatrist is the prevention of violent crime, rather than the acting out of a violent fantasy. This takes longer, but the results may be equally satisfying.

There certainly are ways to avoid violent crime, if one is tuned in to this possibility. There are steps that one can take in different situations to at least minimize the risk of violence. While no guarantee can ever be given to avoid someone losing control and exploding in rage and violence, at least there are possibilities which should be explored to minimize this potential.

An individual with an organic brain syndrome, such as Saul Levenson, who not only killed his own wife, but an innocent hotel keeper, should be followed closely by both his family and treating physicians. There are medications which are similar to the tranquilizers given to schizophrenics. These medications can keep individuals from exploding in violence. They can reduce the amount of paranoid thinking which leads to a belief that others are out to harm the person afflicted with the disease. They can soothe and tranquilize irritable brains. Proper medication can reduce the possibility of not only attacking others, but self-destruction as well. This is something which can be looked for in people with organic impairment and treated.

I have seen a number of cases of individuals with organic brain syndromes, such as Alzheimer's disease, multi-infarct dementia (repeated strokes), hardening of the arteries of the brain, and so on, who have become irritable, agitated and even paranoid as the disease progresses. I have been able to warn the families about this violent behavior increasing in tempo without proper treatment, and they have listened. As a result, I think there have been far fewer risks in these individuals than might otherwise have been the case. While an elderly individual is not usually capable of physically battering someone to death, as was the case with Saul, they are able to get ahold of knives and even guns and, therefore, do not require great physical strength to wreak havoc. Individuals with sado- masochistic fantasies and acting out proclivities require close attention and deserve the interest of our society in general. If an individual, such as the man we called Henry Williams, comes to the attention of the authorities because of hitting women with bricks for sexual gratification, or something else of a sim- ilar bizarre nature, he probably needs to be followed indefinitely.

In California, there is a statute called the Mentally Disordered Sex Offender Act. This is something which may exist, or should prob- ably be considered in other states as well. It means that an individual who is convicted of a sexually-oriented crime is identified and, in fact, registered with the proper authorities. This gives the society an oppor- tunity to monitor individuals with these kinds of problems.

While it might be inconvenient for the individual and may also single out some people who possibly are not harmful to others, it also protects a great many more people from harm to have sex offenders under scrutiny. Should Henry Williams have been under scrutiny all through his life, it is at least possible that he would have been less likely to have committed the final terrible act which put him in jail. The MDSO Act causes people to be registered and requires that they be on probation and remain in treatment for long periods of time. Even after the treatment is completed, they continue to be registered and, therefore, are aware that they are the subject of public and official awareness. In situations of this nature, it is probably true that eternal vigilance is the price of safety. Until we have a better purchase on a method for treating individuals with sexually-oriented disorders, this seems to be our only reasonable means of protecting the greatest number of individual citizens.

The largest number of murders which occur in this country and all around the world are those which happen between husbands and wives, boyfriends and girlfriends, lovers and friends, and intimate acquaintances of every description. There is no question among police authorities that the vast majority of murders are done by people who know the victims extremely well. Murders for profit and murders for political and commercial goals are the rarities, rather than the rule. Serial murders and murders by psychotic individuals, while being extremely dramatic and devastating, are much less common than crimes of passion. In this book we have described several murders relating to wives killing husbands and husbands killing wives, and discussed how they might have been avoided. This, of course, is speculation.

The value of learning among human beings is to apply the knowledge obtained to potential new situations in the future. It has been my experience that through acting as a consultant to the Superior Court, especially in matters, of marital strife and resulting homicides, I have learned something about how to avoid these problems when they arise in other couples. I have used this, I think, to good effect, and can describe several instances in which I believe we have avoided death and destruction. Many of these cases are very similar to the ones cited in this book' with a different result.

Laura G. consulted me because she was plagued by fear that her marriage was going on the rocks and that her husband would become enraged with her because she was engaged in an affair with another man. She was, in fact, carrying on with another man who was very well known to her husband. He was their next-door neighbor. The affair had been going on for six months and, so far, had

escaped the notice of both her husband and her neighbor's wife as well. How they were able to get away with this trick escaped me, but since it also escaped their respective spouses, they were still amorously carrying on.

I pointed out to Laura that it was only a matter of time before one or the other spouse discovered what was happening. She agreed that this was probably true, and was one of the reasons why she consulted me initially. She wanted some way to tell her husband about the problem and possibly to expect a divorce from him, while her neighbor divorced his wife. Then, they might all remarry each other in a happier fashion. I pointed out that this was folly and hardly likely to come to pass. I further indicated that I doubted if her neighbor was as anxious to get a divorce and remarry her as she thought he was. It seemed to me that the best solution was to drop the affair altogether.

It took a number of hours of psychiatric treatment to deal with her motives in getting involved with her neighbor in the first place, especially since the multiple fantasies which she had about this relationship had to be dealt with slowly and carefully. We had to explore both his and her motivations in getting involved in such a dangerous and potentially explosive matter. When she was able to see the possible lethal results of her neurotic activities, she came to agree that it would be best to terminate them all together. This would be better than to further compound the problem by a confession to her husband and risk the ultimate explosion which that would bring on.

One of the ways I was able to help her was to discuss several of the murder cases which had been in the public press. As it happened, the subject was of much local discussion. I indicated to her that she could easily be the topic of the cocktail conversation in a few weeks, either as the victim or as the accused in a murder case. I told her further that it was not unusual for this kind of situation to blow up in one's face. She could just as easily become the subject of front-page headlines as the people whom she read about in yesterday's newspaper.

The important thing to remember in these kinds of situations is that they do happen to ordinary people. Most murders are done by ordinary citizens of middle-class backgrounds. It is the ordinary citizen who gets sucked in more and more into a bizarre situation without realizing it that becomes the focus of our attention in these matters.

The logic of this argument was vividly impressed upon Laura. She did, in fact, cease and desist in her affair after discussing it with her boyfriend. He, too, and possibly even more quickly, understood the gravity of the situation. He agreed to seek solace for his unhappy marriage in fields further away from his home territory. Laura, on the other hand, agreed to work together with me to try to make her marriage work more effectively. Together with her husband, we were in fact able to affect a more amicable, peaceful and non-lethal solution to their mutual problems. So far as I know, at this time, they are still together, and no one is the worse for wear.

Mary T. was a thirty-five-year-old housewife, who was becoming increasingly enraged at her husband because of what she regarded as his unfaithfulness. She was certain that he was carrying on with one of his employees. She had followed him on several occasions to work, and had seen him touching, fondling and, otherwise, becoming intimate with his secretary. She became suspicious of his "business trips" out of town, and eventually hired a detective to check him out when he went to San Francisco for a meeting. The meeting, unfortunately, was not with his business colleagues, but with his secretary. Mary decided that she was being cuckolded, and was unable to tolerate this embarrassment. She began to feel that all of her friends and neighbors knew about this, but her. She decided to punish her husband, and actually bought a gun, pointed it at him, and threatened to shoot him should he transgress in the future. He unhesitatingly denied everything and told her she was crazy. He suggested that she see a psychiatrist to deal with her paranoid delusions.

It became reasonably clear in treatment, however, that Mary was not crazy in the classic sense. She had information which was undeniable, including some intercepted letters from her husband to his lover and vice versa. She had the report of the private detective, which the husband never realized had been rendered. She continued to believe he was carrying on, despite his vehement protestations.

He reluctantly agreed to come in for a session with the psychiatrist when she insisted that he do so. It turned out, of course, that he did not vigorously and vehemently deny the relationship when faced with the evidence obtained by his wife.

Ultimately, it became clear that the marriage itself was not viable, and it was agreed to divorce. The couple divorced with some bitterness, but no violence. No blood was shed, a marriage was dissolved, and both parties are now alive and able to tell the tale. While this is not a happy resolution to a problem in life, it is a far more reasonable one than murder. Moreover, it gives both parties the opportunity to seek more reasonable alliances in the future. The murder of one or the other ends one party's life and destroys the value of the other. While reconciliation in marriage is desirable if it can be achieved, divorce is a far better solution than murder. I have, in fact, advocated it on several occasions in order to avoid a more violent resolution.

Relationships among homosexuals frequently are fraught with explosiveness and rage. Many times, one homosexual individual will accuse the other of infidelity, of "cruising" and soliciting the amorous attention of other men or women. Lyle Q. was such an individual. He was in love with Robert, who was twenty years his junior. Robert was an attractive young man in his mid-twenties, and lived with Lyle Q. because he saw the older man as being "mature, intelligent and thoughtful. This, at least, is what he told him and what Lyle chose to believe. After Robert had, on several occasions, betrayed him, or at least Lyle believed that this was so, Lyle began to develop, in addition to rage and distress, an ulcer. His ulcer was compounded by colitis, and his internist suggested he needed psychiatric intervention.

Lyle reluctantly agreed to see a psychiatrist, and it took only one visit to get him to reveal the cause of his agitation and worry. He described his belief that he was being betrayed by Robert and, ultimately, we got to the real cause of his worry. He knew he was twenty years older than his young lover and not as attractive as he had once been. Robert probably was using him for support, as the younger man was without any visible means of support, nor had any vocation.

Lyle had a successful business and made a good deal of money. He felt used and believed that he was being "toyed with and betrayed" by his friend. Their arguments had frequently been violent. Robert had, on two or three occasions, struck Lyle with his fists. Since Robert was younger and more energetic than Lyle, he was becoming frightened. He feared that Robert might hurt him badly, and he had recently acquired a weapon. He kept a small .22 caliber pistol in his bedstand, and vowed that should Robert attack him again, he would shoot him.

It became clear to me that, in addition to dealing with my patient's gastrointestinal problems, we had matters of even more urgency to handle. I pointed out that the situation with Robert was probably going nowhere. Robert was young, energetic, and had dreams of grandeur. Lyle probably was not going to be enough for him. Living in Palm Springs and "decaying" with "all of the other old relics" was not going to suit him. He needed the bright lights of Los Angeles or San Francisco. He was spending much of his time commuting back and forth to L.

A. anyway, and likely would not remain with his older lover much longer.

We agreed to try to get Lyle to gracefully back away from this scene and to find someone more suitable. This was a difficult resolution for him to accept but, in the light of the alternatives which were discussed, seemed the only reason able one. Reconciliation did not seem to be in the cards. Lyle was not getting any younger, and despite a face lift, still didn't look any younger. Robert was vigorous, energetic and anxious to move on. Lyle finally realized that complaining and arguing with his young friend was not going to change him, and shooting him would not only remove him from circulation, but also remove my patient from society. A search for a new friend might be arduous and tedious and even unrewarding, but it was better than going to jail for the rest of his life. The kinds of people that one meets in San Quentin and Folsom Prisons are not the socially acceptable group that Lyle was used to engaging. You could not have a good conversation about music and art with most of the inmates in penal institutions. He took the graceful way out, gave Robert some money, and signed over the car to him. Robert gratefully departed for points west.

In follow-up, while Lyle has not found the ideal person to suit his needs, he has remained in circulation, and retains a clean conscience. He is not in Folsom penitentiary.

There are similar situations which have arisen which are either more or less dramatic. I have chosen the ones that were obviously lethal because of the potential of weapons causing death. A number of others, however, occur with regularity. If they can be anticipated by the therapist, the principals can be warned in time. This can be extremely rewarding, if negative reward. That is, it is hard to know that you have prevented a killing since it does not, in fact, occur.

Nevertheless, the situations are sufficiently similar to ones in which they have occurred to give at least this psychotherapist the impression that some very specific good has been achieved.

The act of murder creeps up on you. You and I can get gradually sucked into a series of situations, as described in this book, which, at the outset, never seemed to be leading to the final destructive resolution which we have described. An ordinary person is, in fact, capable of killing and, in fact, most of the killings we have described have been done by ordinary people. Each of us is capable of this kind of destructive activity, and each of us is familiar with how to do it.

The popularity of war movies, gangster pictures and "adventure" stories attest to our familiarity with destruction and our vicarious enjoyment of it. As long as it stays in the movies and people like "Dirty Harry" carry them out, no one is any the worse for wear. When it begins to affect our personal lives and touch upon our everyday experiences, much more attention has to be paid. It is then that professional assistance is essential.

There are a number of other murders which have occurred in Palm Springs and environs which were unable to be included in this particular book. Certainly, there will be a number more which will be committed in the future as well. We can't prevent every crime, and we are usually not consulted on most of them.

In addition, there are a number of unsolved murders in the desert, which the police are still investigating. There is the murder of the race track owner, his wife and servant by what appeared to be "professional hit men." The police still have this case open, and have a suspect. Should he finally be apprehended, it may well be that this was a crime for profit and/or for revenge.

There is also the murder of the art dealer and an unfortunate house painter who happened to walk in to the murder scene as the victim was being shot. The police have some suspects in this case as well, and the investigations continue.

Then, there is the murder of the wealthy widow by her young boyfriend, who claims that he was framed by her children so that they could inherit all her money. He says that there are millions at stake, but that's another story, or ...

A NEW WORD FOR MURDER